SIGNOR
DIDO

SIGNOR DIDO

ALBERTO SAVINIO

TRANSLATED BY RICHARD PEVEAR

COUNTERPOINT

BERKELEY

Library of Congress Cataloging-in-Publication Data
Savinio, Alberto, 1891–1952.
[Short stories. Selections. English]
Signor Dido : stories / Alberto Savinio.
pages cm
ISBN 978-1-61902-238-6 (hardback)
I. Title.
PQ4809.H45A2 2014
853'.912—dc23
2013042659

COUNTERPOINT
1919 Fifth Street
Berkeley, CA 94710
www.counterpointpress.com

Printed in the United States of America
Distributed by Publishers Group West

10 9 8 7 6 5 4 3 2 1

Contents

A Note on the Author
and His Book

With the increase of years, the will to work also increases in me
and plans gather ever more thickly in my head. But time restricts
me in the same proportion. What a strange error life is!

—Alberto Savinio

THE STORIES COLLECTED IN *Signor Dido* are among the last works of one of the most gifted and singular Italian writers of the twentieth century. They were published in the newspaper *Corriere della Sera* from 1949 to 1952; the last to be written, "A Mental Journey," was sent to the paper on May 2, 1952, just four days before the author's death. But the collection, which was originally scheduled for publication a few years later, did not come out until 1978.

The stories have the feeling of being last works, though Savinio was only sixty-one when he died (his older brother, the painter Giorgio de Chirico, lived to be ninety). Composed with an extreme economy of means, they are the summing up of a rich and complex life, told now in the first person, now through the figure of Savinio's double, Signor Dido. The circumstances and surroundings are Savinio's. The family members sometimes have the real names of Savinio's family—his wife Maria, his children Angelica and Ruggero—and sometimes alliterating alternatives like Marta, Armida, and Rinaldo. (In one story an anti-Dido also appears, a certain Signor Dodi, who represents everything that Dido is not.) The stories contain haunting premonitions and at times a piercing solitude, but they are all graced with Savinio's high comic sense, his fine self-humor, and that stylistic irony which, as he once said, is both a mask for modesty and "a subtle way of insinuating oneself into the secret of things."

Savinio's mother was a baroness of the Genoese nobility; his father was a Sicilian baron who worked as a civil engineer constructing railways in Greece. Savinio was born in Athens. With the death of his father in 1905, when Savinio was fourteen, the baroness moved the family to Munich, where he studied music under Max Reger, while his brother attended the fine arts academy. They moved to Paris in 1910, and the young men soon became part of the Apollinaire-Picasso circle. It was there that de Chirico painted the first "metaphysical paintings" and Savinio gave concerts and published his first writings. In 1915 the brothers returned to Italy for military service. In the postwar years they moved to Rome, where in 1924 they collaborated with Luigi Pirandello in founding the Teatro d'Arte, and Savinio met his future wife, the actress Maria Morino. They moved to Paris in 1927, where Savinio, who had abandoned music after the war, continued to write and also took up painting. The family (now including their daughter Angelica) returned to Italy definitively in 1933. From then on, Savinio's production flourished more and more richly in various fields: painting, fiction, journalism, biography, criticism, playwriting, stage and costume design, philosophical reflection, political commentary. In relation to fascism, as he wrote in his *Nuova Enciclopedia*, he once proposed "the creation of a league whose members would pledge to remain unaware of Mussolini and never speak his name. If more people had the will, the resoluteness, and above all the 'hygienic concern' necessary to keep such a pledge," he added, "the rise of men like Mussolini and Hitler would be like a balloon trying to rise in an airless space."

All the phases of Savinio's past are present in the stories of *Signor Dido*. His world is laced with memories, which erupt suddenly, unexpectedly, in the midst of the most banal circumstances. Savinio-Dido is interviewing a young man who is going to do some typing for him; the young man demonstrates how he sits at the typewriter; the angle of his position suddenly reminds the author of the tragic death of a famous music-hall performer he had seen in Paris before the First World War, and he is briefly transported back into that world. There are many similar moments in the book. And yet, paradoxically, we are told in another story, "Signor Dido keeps the door of his memories shut. Memories are dangerous. They bring shame and remorse with them. Signor Dido opens it very rarely." He does not dote on the past; his memories have nothing to do with nostalgia. On the contrary, "things in formation attract Signor Dido's attention more lovingly than things already formed and petrified." In the first story in our collection, caught in the dark during a momentary power failure, Dido has a vision that takes him out of the "trap" of his everyday life in Rome: "Amidst the green valley sparkling with flowers flows the clear and silent stream. What freedom! What freedom to go! To go over the fields. To go down the rivers. To go across those blue mountains, shining at their summits with the last spring snows. To go over the white clouds that pass in flocks. To go into the infinite depths of the sky." And in the last story, he finally does *go*.

A cumulative self-portrait, then, but much more as well. The

world of *Signor Dido* is a world of intersections and transforma-
tions. The trivia of daily life yield to the visionary; reality suddenly turns fantastic; fantasy is interrupted by a discussion of
etymology; the ordinary is transformed by myth; the myth de-
volves into satire. Savinio's method of composition is avowedly
digressive. Writers can be divided into two sorts: those who revel
in puns and those who abhor them. Savinio revels in puns; he
calls them "extemporaneous philology." He loves the accident
that produces a new meaning, typing errors, grammatical "mis-
takes" that lead him somewhere he had not thought of going. He
undercuts his narrative but maintains it at the same time, and the
reader's "willing suspension of disbelief" is replaced by a participation in the composition itself. This is all a stylistic rendering of
the freedom he celebrated in that momentary vision during the
power failure.

In the introduction to a new edition of Tommaso Campanella's
utopian treatise *The City of the Sun* (first published in 1602),
Savinio comments: "Working in this utopian atmosphere, I have
ended by believing utopianly that my readers have all overcome
the prejudice of seriousness, which spreads so much darkness
over matters of culture and life in general, and know now that
seriousness is an obstacle and a limitation, and therefore a form
of unintelligence." His own writing, as in the final distillation of
Signor Dido, is always blessedly free of that prejudice.

—Richard Pevear

SIGNOR
DIDO

Signor Dido's Afternoon

IN THE AFTERNOON, THE HOUSE surrounding Signor Dido is a trap. Usually the morning is freer. But today even the morning went badly. Signor Dido woke up with a slight headache. He took a pill. The pain hid itself behind a veil, but the veil also extended to Signor Dido's head, his arms, his legs. In the newspaper the usual void, the usual tedium. In the world the usual stupidity. The mail brought him an invitation to the concert of a Hungarian pianist and a circular urging people to contribute with prayers and offerings to a Votive Temple of Peace. Two telephone calls: one for his son Rodolfino, who at that hour was in school; the other from the Vasco Company, requesting payment of the balance for a supply of firewood from last year. Even the imagination was sterile this morning. Signor Dido's minute handwriting had barely reached the bottom of the first page when the voice of Paolina announced from the doorway: "It's on the table." Agnese and Rodolfino were already immersed in the pasta. There was also Matteo, Agnese's "fiancé," and Signora Mariangela, Signor Dido's sister-in-law. The place of Signora Matilde, Signor Dido's wife, was empty, because Signora Matilde had suffered a synovial discharge in her left knee and was in bed. Signor Dido would have liked to speak of lofty and poetic things—would have liked above all to speak of himself and hear himself spoken of—and instead

3

he had to be silent. The conversation at the table is dominated by young Matteo. The soul of Agnese's fiancé tends towards mechanics, and he can tell the cylinder capacity of an automobile by listening to the sound of the motor, just as a musician can tell the notes of a chord without looking at the keyboard. All that's left of the soup is the grease in the bottoms of the bowls. Paolina comes in carrying the main dish and dragging her big, aching feet. A sound darts across the avenue. Young Matteo shouts: "Eight cylinders." To which Mariangela, slow and severe, replies: "Just as I said!" At Signor Dido's table, Signora Mariangela represents popular wisdom descended from the mountains of the Abruzzi; this wisdom is expressed in the affirmation: "Just as I said," which Signora Mariangela repeats for all purposes, above all in regard to things, and they are many, which she has never heard of. Into the wisdom of Signora Mariangela the notion of thrift also enters, extended to the alimentary field. Signora Mariangela ostentatiously eats what the others have refused, the green leaves of cauliflower, the sinewy parts of meat, the heads of fish. Signor Dido would like, above all at the noon meal, to eat lightly and in conformity with the diet for diabetics. But in Signor Dido's house, the arguments of Signor Dido are not taken seriously. The meal, today as well, has been heavy and full of starches. Current in the Dido household are such precepts as the following: "Growing children cannot *skip* the soup." Signor Dido is weak. And what courage, to eliminate the reasons for reproaching oneself, above all for pitying oneself . . . Today as well Signor Dido yielded to the abundant pasta, rich in carbohydrates. And afterwards he felt sleepy. And he slept. And after sleeping he had to go to the bathroom and do everything he had done in the morning. And when he was in a condition to sit down at the desk, it was already evening and he had to turn on the light. He read over three times, attentively, the page he had written that morning, to get back into its spirit; after which, without much fervor, he drew a small 2 on a new sheet of paper and began to write. He had gone a couple of lines when the door to the studio opened and a man appeared on the threshold, bearing behind him, like a cloak of eternity, all the darkness of the corridor. He did not linger on the threshold, but came in. Came in with his head high. Inexorable. He was blind. Two days earlier, Signor Dido had telephoned Signor Tottuccio, the piano tuner, asking him to come and fix the hammer of the low C, which had broken, but meanwhile he had forgotten the phone call. Signor Tottuccio's entrance was an unexpected apparition. "Here I am, *professore*,"[1] said Signor Tottuccio, advancing resolutely and looking up with his blank eyes. Signor Tottuccio knew no obstacles. He was about to bump into the desk, but within a finger of the sharp corner, he stopped. Suddenly. If you look at Signor Tottuccio straight on, you don't see the guide who controls his confident steps. Small of stature and hidden behind the mass of her husband, Signora Tottuccio holds on to the folds of his jacket with both hands, as if it were a steering wheel. Signor Dido's piano was quickly flayed by the expert hands of Signora Tottuccio, shamelessly revealing its stripy golden viscera. The cover of the keyboard was placed on the daybed. The scores passed from the top of the piano to the easy chair. Signor Dido's armchair was occupied by Signora Tottuccio, who, while her husband, inspired in his darkness, worked on the instrument's innards, sat waiting, her eyes bent over a yellow book. There was no seat left for Signor Dido. But even if there had been one, Signor Dido would still have left the studio, because his irreducible timidity would consent to cohabitation only with persons of consummate intimacy. Besides, in the studio the tried and retried notes began to strike repeatedly, insupportably, and from the person of Signora Tottuccio, tiny and in a state of repose as she was, the smell of sebaceous secretions began to spread. Signor Dido left.

He left the studio but not the trap.

Now Signor Dido is in the corridor. He opens a door to the left. The children's room. Four or five faces turn suddenly: little, astonished, hostile, nasty. Like five creatures, five little monsters. Signor Dido does not know who these children are. Rodolfino's friends, no doubt. He does not understand what they are doing, bunched up in that corner. And they have covered the light. He does not even have time to see if Rodolfino is among these boys. Timid, fearful, Signor Dido hurriedly closes the door. An "Excuse me" dies in his teeth.

A trap.

He opens another door. Matilde is in bed. In the faint light of the shaded bulb, suffering eyes look at him without brightness, with reproach. He, in this house, is the cause of everything. Therefore also of the synovial discharge. Signor Dido shuts the door again.

Where to take refuge?

The third door is to the dining room. The heat does not reach that far. The room is like ice. But what else is left? Signor Dido opens . . . There, by the window, drinking up the last glow of the winter twilight, Estella, the cook, pushes the piece of cloth under the vertical needle of the machine and rocks the pedal with her foot.

A trap.

Where to go? . . . Try the "facilities." Despite the freezing temperature, despite the dampness of the evening, see about the terrace in the courtyard. Signor Dido opens the door to the kitchen. Beside the icebox in winter disuse, big as a half-inflated

Montgolfier on her low seat, Paolina, her aching feet immersed in a tub of warm salted water, turns to look at him with the eyes of a bitch that has just given birth.

Signor Dido withdraws to the front hall. Sits on an extremely hard little bench made of wood and straw, on which coats are usually thrown. From down the corridor an F minor chord rings out again and again . . . The smell of fish glue, which will be used to glue the hammer of the low C, spreads through the house.

A trap.

And if he leaves the house? If he leaves the trap?

On his feet Signor Dido is wearing thick fur-lined slippers with ears. On his legs his "house" trousers, American army issue, bought by his wife that past summer in Livorno from the leftovers in Tòmbolo.[2] On his shoulders an old doublet knitted by his sister-in-law. And he hadn't shaved that morning. So as not to be tempted to go out. To force himself to work. Alfieri-style.[3] But how work in this trap?

Facing the hard little bench is a wardrobe. Signor Dido opens the wardrobe, takes out a pair of shoes. To substitute them for the slippers, Signor Dido leans his back against the wall and raises a foot. While he is in this stork-like position, Paolina comes moaning from the "facilities," goes down the corridor, bumps into him with her enormous and soft breast as she passes by, and almost knocks him over. From there, now, an arpeggio chord in B major rings out. Again and again . . .

Before venturing onto the street, Signor Dido judges it prudent to visit the bathroom for a moment.

Inside the door, "something" warm and agile, damp and soft, jumps on him. It is Gidi, the little mongrel bitch, in an affectionate mood, locked in the bathroom by the boys so that she would not disturb them at their incomprehensible games.

If Gidi were a male, it would be different. But how to do in front of a female what Signor Dido has come to the bathroom to do?

Signor Dido opens the door and tries nicely, then firmly, to make Gidi leave. But the little bitch is starved for affection. She makes extremely high leaps around Signor Dido, as if the floor tiles were red hot; she nips at the trousers from Tòmbolo.

Yielding to his powerlessness, overcoming his modesty, Signor Dido approaches the toilet, places himself so that his back is turned to Gidi. Anxious but functional.

Agile and silent, the little bitch circles around the toilet; all at once Signor Dido finds her in front of him. He turns with a jerk, hurriedly puts things right . . . Too hurriedly. Dampness runs down his leg, turns cold.

A trap.

Signor Dido returns with tense steps to the front hall. Slips on his overcoat, winds a scarf around his neck to hide his lack of a tie. Opens the front door, and from the threshold, he who lives on the ground floor sees people crowding under the gateway, obscure, unknown, before sheets of rain falling silvery and straight and beating on the shiny pavement in liquid spatters.

A trap.

Signor Dido returns to the extremely hard little bench, and as he bends to sit down, the lights suddenly go out all over the house.

From there, repeated scales and trills, arpeggios and chords echo in the darkness. Light or no light, what's the difference to a blind tuner?

In the darkness, Signor Dido reflects.

Amidst the green valley sparkling with flowers flows the clear and silent stream. What freedom! What freedom to go! To go over the fields. To go down the rivers. To go across those blue mountains, shining at their summits with the last spring snows.

To go over the white clouds that pass in flocks. To go into the infinite depths of the sky.

The valleys and mountains are full of people. Gods perhaps. Gods certainly. Invisible but given away by their voices. By the choral song that passes like a sublime, harmonious wind.

The lights come back on: the valley is extinguished, the river is extinguished, the mountains are extinguished, the sky is extinguished.

Even the arpeggios are extinguished. The stupid, idiotic arpeggios of the blind tuner testing the keyboard. Signor Dido pricks up his ears: the pelting of the rain has stopped.

Signor Dido opens the front door. The gateway is empty. People and vehicles hurry up and down the bright street.

Signor Dido closes the door.

To go.

But where? To whom?

A trap.

A Visit from K . . .

THE ROOM THAT I'VE TURNED INTO a studio in my residence is a "conclusion." Brain or intestine, as the case may be. Here the house ends. There's no going beyond it. Outside the window begins the world of "the others": the street, passers-by, vehicles, and, unfortunately, the uninterrupted, repeated, sputtering, "useless" passage of all the young lads of this "elegant" quarter, mounted singly, or in twos, or in threes, on *birotae igneo liquido incitatae* (*Pontifex dixit*).[1]

A corridor, in direct communication with the front hall and the outside door, leads like a canal to my studio-brain, to my studio-intestine. Between studio and corridor, a door with a frosted glass window acts as a diaphragm.

(Yesterday.) I was in my studio. Late morning. The young lads' *birotae* were passing through my brain like ineffable saws. Unexpectedly, a yellow brightness lit up the frosted diaphragm from behind: the sign of an "important" passage down the corridor. (The light was lit in the corridor only for "important" passages, or else, early in the morning, for "the cleaning.") Two voices were advancing along it: the voice of my wife, and a deep male voice. Who could it be?

"No. It won't disturb him at all."

My wife's voice was by now at the threshold: too close for me to be able to inform her that this person, whoever it was, was indeed disturbing me, and very much so.

A "complete" wife combines wife and mother in herself. On that side I'm in good order. My mother, to the last, and when I was already a forty-six-year-old child, never consulted me before having me do what she, in her judgment, had decided was good for me to do. She placed me Hitlerianly before the accomplished fact. For the dispensers of absolute good, freedom of judgment equals freedom to be wrong. And wives, mothers, dictators are so many dispensers of absolute good. The example, moreover, comes from on high.

The door opened.

"Signor K . . . has come to pay his respects."

"Good morning, *professore* . . . Am I disturbing you? . . . My respects . . . Don't trouble yourself . . . I'll stay a minute, then take my leave . . . You always have so much to do . . . Your time is precious . . ."

Why "*professore*"? I'm not a *professore*. Those who call me *professore* and *dottore* prove to me, in the first place, that in their judgment my name alone is not enough to personalize me, and thus make a *gaffe*; they commit a falsehood, in the second place, because I have no right to any academic title; in the third place, they erect a barrier of embarrassment between me and them-selves, which deprives our relations of any possibility either of usefulness or of pleasure.

But how maintain one's aggressiveness, or even defensiveness, before this big candle dressed in a shabby overcoat, his face and hands furrowed with tears of wax?

The K above, followed by a three-point ellipsis, is the initial of a German surname which, in Italian, sounds like something indecent, and therefore I could not write it out in full. The name that precedes the unutterable surname is Erick.

I got to know K . . . many years ago. (Twenty.) In Paris. He was a friend of a friend of mine. At that time K . . . was a candidate for suicide: for suicide *on a prearranged date*. It was then March 15. (After twenty years I cannot guarantee the exactness of the date. But what matter? It's only an example.) He announced that he would kill himself a month later: on April 15.

During the month of "waiting," we were not troubled at all. Perhaps we did not believe in the sincerity of the statement. Perhaps out of indifference. Perhaps for that reason which we are usually ashamed to admit—that another person's life is of little value to us. Above all that of an almost unknown person.

Gabriele D'Annunzio,[2] some years earlier, had forecast his own death several times. Of the publicity purpose of these forecasts no one had any doubt. Here it was different. It concerned quite another type of man.

April 15 came and passed; more days passed. None of us was interested in whether K . . . had kept his promise or not. Then, by chance, we learned that he had not kept it. Out of fear? . . . No. He had only put it off to the next month. Without a trace of laughter. With inexorable seriousness. Besides, how imagine an act of K . . .'s not marked by inexorable seriousness? K . . .'s case is one of those that have demonstrated to me most profoundly the perfect interdependence between seriousness and stupidity on the one hand, and, on the other, between seriousness and madness.

(Today.) K . . . is strolling around my studio. "Inspecting" my studio. Looking at each object. Looking closely at it. Examining it. More than looking at it, sniffing it. Perhaps searching for a favorable place to . . . Like dogs. It had not escaped me, moreover, that in the transformation that had come over him during the time in which we had lost sight of each other, the olfactory had taken a clear predominance over the other senses.

(Then.) He kept putting off his own death month by month. Like putting off a departure. Like putting off a trip. Of the announced death of Erick K . . . we no longer thought. We lost sight of him.

There are two K . . .s, Erick and a sister: Mariasibilla. Both children of a general of the ex-Austro-Hungarian empire, governor of a maritime and military city. The miserable end of the Austro-Hungarian empire was prolonged in these two "victims." Old people now, in whom the stigmata of orphanism have not been erased. Pale orphans. Shaken by a feeble madness. Vienna. The Prater. Franz Joseph. The Sacher restaurant.[3]

I met K . . . again in Italy. He no longer talked of killing himself. Of two solutions, he had chosen the worse: to live.

Fifty years old, he had set himself to studying for a degree in jurisprudence. A "guarantee for the future," he said. He was helped by a young lawyer who lodged in a furnished room. One day K . . . arrived at the lawyer's, but the lawyer had gone out. K . . . waited. The lawyer was late. K . . . went away.

He came back the next day. He was met by the landlady. After his visit the day before, ten thousand lire, kept in a drawer, had disappeared.

Under this accusation, which, like an enormous white crow, unexpectedly descended upon this man of wax and clung to him, K . . . behaved himself in such fashion that in the end, to make him leave that house, it was necessary to call in four strong men, who carried him between them, each holding one extremity, like a sack in which a furious octopus is struggling.

From Austria, from the broken-up paternal home, from the splendors *d'antan*,[4] Erick and Mariasibilla came by stages to

Rome, to a wretched village outside the porta San Giovanni. With them they brought a grand piano, once magnificent and powerful, some splendid pieces of silver plate, and a big drawing by Vincenzo Gemito.[5]

I've seen it. It's the head of a Roman girl. A stern goddess of the people. And the extraordinary draftsman's line, so strong, so sure, so artfully interlaced, has difficulty restraining the full, profound life of this earthly divinity.

Before the yellowed and decayed teeth of this faithful member of the great family K . . ., Mariasibilla sits and, accompanying herself with hands like the claws of a crustacean, sings the sweet and profound Lieder of Brahms, turning them sour. Exotic clothing, Mongolian capes, calf-length boots, enormous bell-shaped gowns, *toilettes* in which, despite the faint heat of the body in its musical excitement, the odor of the illustrious sweat of court balls reawakens. Escorted by her voice, the singer's heart, her viscera, her soul, rusty and creaking organs, issue from their dark recesses; and the voice, which passion drives now right, now left, flaps like a window blind left hanging from a single hook and shaken by a storm.

The four strong men will carry the sack with the furious octopus in it down the stairs, load it into a taxi, and unload it at the door of a hospital.

(Now.) K . . . is sitting in front of me. Body leaning forward, neck tense, chin thrust out. As if to *partake* of my person. And of the desk I'm sitting behind. And of the various things placed on the desk. And I feel that, to partake even better, he would like to touch me, touch the desk, touch the various things. This man has need of "contacts."

He says:

"Ten days ago they gave me the last electro-shock. I have a

month off. I'm profiting from it to renew contacts. May I see your works, *professore*? I had lost all memory. Now it's gradually coming back to me. And of the gentleman your brother? . . . I'm ready to pay. Not much, to be honest. Is it true that there is free admission to the Galeria d'Arte Moderna? Maybe you need a special permit. In that case I'll show my student papers. I'm a student. A student of law. Excuse me, *professore*. I'll take my leave. Now I can tell you this. I had no great esteem for Italian science. Now it's different. Now I know. Electro-shock is the discovery of a genius. I'm not making believe. I have experience. In Vienna I was two years in the madhouse. They gave me insulin. A great professor. Horrible! Horrible! They flop you into bed like a dead man. Electro-shock is no comparison."

His "student papers" were two years spent in a Vienna madhouse, and coma from insulin. In this alone the Italian doctors were mistaken in his regard, in persistently considering him a schizophrenic (and him so learned in mental illnesses), when he is a fixated depressive.

K . . . gets up from the armchair and moves forward, leaning his body across the desk, as if he wants to touch my face with his.

I did not insist so much on preferring depressive fixation to schizophrenia, nor on the self-love, the pride contained in that preference, until I remembered that schizophrenia leads to brutishness, while depressive fixation is an intellectualistic form of madness. Crazy, yes, but in the most worthy form. K . . . is an intellectual. A *phantasm* of an intellectual. In Vienna, many years ago, he was a student of Schönberg. And now?

"I've decided."

"In what way?"

"Dreams. Vonderful, extraordinary dreams. All my life I've had vonderful, extraordinary dreams. What I compose in my dreams, in poetry, in painting, in music, is much more beautiful, much more pure above all, than what I do awake—than what all of you do awake."

In uttering this phrase, he turns spiteful.

"You should write down your dreams."

"Dreams can't be written down. Shouldn't be. It would be absurd. Dreams can only be written down in dreams."

My wife comes into the studio from time to time on some pretext, "checks things out," and leaves again.

"Now, after the electro-shock, my dreams are different. Full of blood. I dream of men with tails. And I kill them. I kill a dozen per dream. These dreams give me an extraordinary euphoria."

At these words, my wife comes into the studio, but this time she places herself at my side and no longer moves. Marriage is such complicity! Even facing a poor man of wax who is being consumed, consumed, consumed inside and out. Marriage, an association for attack and defense, is the nucleus of egotistical, wicked, armed society.

At intervals K . . . says again: "*Professore*, your time is precious. I'll take my leave." But he doesn't move. He goes on talking. Either in monosyllables, or in paired words, separated pair by pair. His body leaning towards me. The force of concentration, the great will of persuasion, is manifest on his forehead, in his eyes. As if I were opposing a wall of doubt to his words. What wouldn't I give to convince him that I'm convinced! Full of tears behind the wrinkled skin of his face. The desperate pain of not managing to make himself understood—of not managing to persuade me.

And I understand. I understand perfectly. I understand profoundly. I understand those brief rending sounds. Those sounds that escape in a burst from his gray lips—from his blotting-paper lips. They fly a little. Drop down. Followed at a short distance by more rending sounds . . . A discourse in fragments.

And I understand something else as well. I understand that these words in separate pairs, this posture of the body, this head, this thrust-out chest, this desperate will to convince me, this need to "renew contacts," are the condition of a shipwrecked man. Of a shipwrecked man drifting aimlessly. And, today, the raft towards which this desperate man stretches his hands—today, that raft is me. Tomorrow it will be my "gentleman" brother. The day after tomorrow it will be the Galeria d'Arte Moderna. The sea is not stormy. It is calm. Extremely calm. "Seems" extremely calm. Like oil. But a profound, inexorable, invisible movement of this extremely calm sea carries the shipwrecked man further away, always further away. And it's in vain that the man of wax holds out his hands of wax, down the carpus of which fat tears of wax worm their way.

It is the raft, then, that should move, should go to meet the shipwrecked man, move to rescue the shipwrecked man.

He says once again: "Your time is precious, *professore*. I'll take my leave." But this time, unexpectedly, he gets to his feet. It's so quiet I can hear the breath of relief in my wife's throat.

I follow him down the corridor, escorted by my conjugal guard.

A brief pause at the door, and a brief alarm. A last cascade of paired words. Fear of something . . . Of what?

The door, rapidly and silently, closes on the back of the man of wax.

From behind the window, in hiding, I see him moving off under a fine rain.

He's not walking: he's being carried by the sea, black, invisible. Which separates him from his "contacts." Which carries him far away. To the great shipwreck.

I—his "raft" for that day—could save him.

I don't move.

What swine! . . . And you call yourselves good Christians . . .

Muse

I HAVE TO MAKE A TYPEWRITTEN COPY of the French version of a book I wrote, and have been looking for a typist. Not an easy search. I've heard it said that everyone in Italy knows French: my personal experience shows that few know it.

Three days ago, at last, the longed-for typist presented himself in my house. A neat and extremely orderly young man. A gray suit, a double-breasted jacket, a pince-nez, a very trim haircut, the pious face of a devoted son and the consolation of his parents. A face, I was about to say, such as is not seen anymore.

And not only a good son, but a good husband.

"So young and already married?"

"Yes. And I have a fourteen-month-old baby."

Even a good father, then.

My young typist told me his life in brief. He was born in France, of an Italian father and a French mother. He came to Rome four years ago. Here in Rome he found a beautiful and good young woman. They fell in love; they were united at the foot of the altar.

"My wife," the young typist told me, "is also my cousin. The daughter of one of my father's brothers who stayed in Italy. Before the marriage was decided, two doctors examined the relations of both parties. They found no defects on either side. Our baby is wonderful."

It was a very beautiful day. The young typist looked at the sky through the window of my studio. He added: "Today my wife and son have gone to spend the day in Ostia. I'm alone in the house. I work from seven in the morning till ten in the evening. What a joy to have a baby in the house!"

My young typist loves his work. He speaks of typing as Einstein does of curved space. He divides typists into typists who work with their hands alone and typists who work with their hands and their head. Extremely rare. He is one of them.

He says to me: "I type with all ten fingers. I never look at the keyboard."

He accompanies word with deed. He pulls out a chair, sits down, brings his knees together, rests his hands on an imaginary keyboard, and turns his head to an imaginary page, placed to his left on an imaginary reading stand.

I look at him. I remember.

Fragson was the same: sitting at right angles on a swivel stool, his hands spread over the keyboard of the piano, his face to the public that crowded the hall of the Alhambra.[1]

Many times, in Paris, in the years from 1910 to 1914, I had seen Fragson, the songwriter, sit like that on the stage of the Alhambra. The theater, I believe, no longer exists.

Fragson had a father and a mistress. Fragson's father was in love with his son's mistress. One day, out of jealousy, he killed his own son. It was the spring of 1914. The funeral took place in the afternoon. The cortège left the church of Saint-Philippe-du-Roule. Behind the hearse came a long line of landaus, which transported, in tears, Mayol, Dranem, la Mistinguett, the stars of the *café chantante*. The cortège gradually swelled with seamstresses, milliners, salesgirls and salesmen who came in swarms from the shops, the laboratories of fashion, for the repast. One of them struck up a *refrain* by Fragson. In a short time the immense procession became an immense chorus. The songwriter, like a general in a funeral procession, went to his final rest accompanied by his own songs.

I showed the young typist the pages I had typed out myself, destined for recopying by his agile and expert fingers. He looked at them with commiseration. A work written in this fashion! There are no margins. The lines go across and down right to the bottom of the page. The reader has no desire to read. He will get tired and give up reading. The typist, however, will produce a work by the rules of art. Nice margins above, below, and to the sides. Finally, he will give it to his trusted binder for binding.

I am hushed and admiring. This young typist devotes the same love to his typing as a bibliophile does to his bibliophilia.

What does a bibliophile feel? . . . I'll never know. Unless I, too, one day begin to love books not as things to read, but as things to look at. Or rather to look after.

Before going off, taking my unworthy typescript with him, the young typist leaves me his name and telephone number, which I, as an orderly man, attach with a thumbtack to the doorjamb of my bookcase.

The name of my young typist is Musa.

In the afternoon, my friend Fausto came into my studio, saw the name Musa on the doorjamb of the bookcase followed by a telephone number, and said to me: "I see you're connected with the Muse by telephone. Felicitations."

Who thinks of the Muse anymore?

I ought to be in relations with the Muse. Even if not telephonic. Even with several of the Muses. And maybe with all of them. Except, perhaps, for Urania. Although . . .

Once the poet received the faculty of poeticizing directly from the Muse, and therefore did not begin a poem without first invoking the Muse. And we have the *Menin àeide Theà*; we have the *Andra moi ennepe Mousa*; we have the *Tu spira al petto mio celesti ardori.*[2] Dante himself, at one place in his poem, invokes the dispenser of poetic furor, though in another place he calls the divinities to whom these dispensers belong false and deceitful. But now, silence.

This, too, is an effect of the displacement of the wellsprings of poetry. Once the poet thought of these wellsprings as very far away from him, and ideally traveled enormous distances in order to drink from them. Now, and precisely from Baudelaire on, the poet knows that he will see nothing outside, and that he can trust only in what he will draw from his own depths.

The displacement of the wellsprings of poetry that has taken place is far less well known than we think. Many, out of habit, still believe in inspiration. A young doctor, intelligent, cultivated, and moreover given to the study of metaphysics, asked me a few days ago if there is any difference between the way I feel at the moment when I am about to begin a literary work and the state of trance.

It may be that in other times inspiration warmed the poet like a ray of sunlight. When the poet had well-founded reasons for believing in the actual existence of that warming ray. But now . . .

Now, waiting for that ray is a waste of time.

Stendhal, in his *Pages d'Italie*,[3] tells us: "At twenty, I took it into my head to become a writer. Every morning at eight I sat down at my desk, a sheet of blank paper in front of me and a pen in my hand, and waited for inspiration. At noon inspiration had still not come, so I got up and went to have lunch." Stendhal wrote these things at fifty, when he no longer waited for inspiration and with extraordinary ease filled page after inspired page.

There has been a profound change in the world: even in the supply centers of poetic furor.

Don't forget the change.

Parents and Children

TODAY, AT THE TABLE, MY DAUGHTER complained to her mother and me about the antipathy that we, her parents, show towards her friends of both sexes, and had shown to her little playmates when she was still a child. She added: "I make a point of not inviting my friends to the house, knowing so well how badly you'll treat them."

I was about to deny it, but I didn't. My daughter's words had enlightened me. They had clarified a feeling in me that until now had been obscure. And what they clarified most of all was the analogy that suddenly appeared to me between this feeling of mine and an identical feeling which for some time I had recognized in my daughter: the antipathy she has for my and her mother's friends.

We're at the table, as a family, united in love, and behind that veil, we are mute enemies on a silent battlefield.

The reasons for this war are the same: the will to affirm yourself, the will to deny your neighbor and, if possible, to annihilate him. Whoever it may be. Even your own father, even your own child. And if the will to annihilate your own father or your own child rarely reveals itself, that is not because it isn't there but because it is overlaid by another will: that of affirming yourself through your own father or your own child and, beyond that,

27

through relatives, friends, through all those who are or whom we believe are part of ourselves, an extension of ourselves, a development of our own possibilities.

At the table, my daughter's words had revealed this usually hidden and silent will at one stroke.

Nobody spoke. We all felt the pricking of conscience under our seats.

Which of us is entirely alone? Each of us has a maniple, or a cohort, or even an army of persons by means of which he reinforces himself, extends himself, expands himself. The force of association is that much greater in the young, the more recent is the discovery in themselves of this force, its usefulness, its possibilities.

Hence that most strict, most active, most fanatical jealousy that unites my children to their friends (parts of themselves), and to their teachers, and to all that constitutes their "personal" world; hence the jealousy, though more loose, that unites me to my friends—I who also know how to fight alone; I who also know *not* to fight; I who am also aware of the vanity of fighting.

There are four of us at the table: a family; and behind each of us a little army is drawn up—invisible.

Rarely does the presence of this militia manifest itself; rarely does this militia have occasion to manifest itself. So complex, so various, so different, so contrary are the feelings in the heart of a single family: that mess.

But any reason at all, and the most unexpected at that, can spark a clash or even a most cruel battle. And the invisible troops go into action.

The most indirect of combats. The armies, here more than elsewhere, are passive—and indifferent—instruments. But this most indirect of combats, fought by invisible armies, is in truth the most direct of combats, fought between the most visible adversaries: husband and wife, parents and children.

The combat between parents and children is more bitter, because the children bring to it an enormous load of personal interests, a whole future of them; and the parents for their part have to defend themselves, defend the field against the threat of dispossession, against the "humiliating" danger of substitution.

And if the war between parents and children almost never ends in a fatal way, that is because at a certain point, when the battle is about to get rough, the parents and children separate; the children abandon the parents and go their own way; they understand the uselessness, the absurdity of combat with adversaries with whom, at bottom, they have nothing in common.

The battle between parents and children—the not always silent battle between parents and children—though ended not by the victory of one of the parties, but by a peaceful abandoning of the field, has its epinicium in a closer, more profound, more passionate union of the parents.

If silver anniversaries and golden anniversaries are celebrated, with even greater reason we should celebrate the new and more solemn anniversary once the children, having become adult, having left their training period behind, having become conscious of the need for a different strategy, abandon the parents and set out on their own way, towards the only true and fruitful battles, which are those that are fought between people of the same generation.

Because matrimony, that poetic song of generation (if the pun be permitted), is a pact bound with sacred ties between a man and a woman of the same generation, against other generations, against other people, all of them, including their own children. Once the children leave, the union between husband and wife is purified of its practical reason (procreation); it withdraws into its own pure reason; it enters into the condition of poetry.

One point remained obscure to me. Why this antipathy of mine for my daughter's friends, little men and women whom I do not know and have almost never seen; why this antipathy of my daughter's for her mother's friends and mine, men and women whom my daughter rarely sees, and with whom she has no common affections, feelings, tastes, interests?

I understood.

Friends, in this case, are a way of playing off the cushions (a term from billiards).

The empire of the good, in spite of so many transmutations of values, and though the reasons that first established that empire have weakened greatly and are becoming more and more confused—the empire of the good still has so much force, so much authority, that it does not allow a son to say, or even think, "I dislike my father," nor a father to say, or even think, "I dislike my son." But there is antipathy between fathers and sons. And even hatred. All the more antipathy, all the more hatred, insofar as the conditions for antipathy and hatred are much more frequent between those who love each other and who are united not only by love but by a common life, by common means, by a common affection for people and things, by common habits. Antipathy and hatred do not exclude sympathy and love, just as sympathy and love do not exclude antipathy and hatred. On the contrary. A strange cohabitation, but cohabitation all the same. And they either alternate, or one gains the upper hand over the other, or one hides the other—hides *behind* the other, as most often happens, despite the will to the good that we put into it, that we know we should put into it, that we feel a duty to put into it—that we sense the convenience of putting into it. And there is antipathy and hatred—there is "even" antipathy and hatred—of children for parents and parents for children behind love, behind great love, behind the greatest love; but since this antipathy and hatred cannot be given directly and openly to those it is destined for, the antipathy and hatred go, by an automatic transfer, and unbeknownst to the interested parties, to those who represent the "continuation" of the children, the continuation of the parents: to the friends of the children, to the friends of the parents.

The deepest ground of the drama of passion.

Family

WE SIT DOWN AT THE TABLE TO EAT: myself, my wife, my daughter, my son. Tomorrow I will be fifty-eight, on the fifth of this coming September my wife will be fifty, my daughter Angelica will be twenty-one at the end of this month, and my son Ruggero will be fifteen on the twenty-second of this coming December. And we sit down at the table to eat together. The same food . . . Absurd!

Absurd that individuals of different ages and different generations should eat the same food: absurd first of all that individuals of different ages and different generations should live together. I repeat a figure that has already reached maturity: how can you play Handel's *Largo* and a polka at the same time?

A double absurdity: biological and spiritual.

Who is surprised at this absurdity? Who cares about it?

Nobody.

Nobody is surprised at this absurdity, nobody cares about it, because *nobody sees* this absurdity. And nobody sees this absurdity, because this absurdity *is hidden behind a taboo*: the family. And if ever someone—a very rare case—notices this absurdity, he also will not point it out, for fear that, by pointing it out, he will shatter the "unity" of the family.

But where on earth is this unity?

Once everything was a unity. The world, a unity, was subdivided into so many lesser unities. And one of those unities, one of the most important, the most faithful to the model, was the family.

I came in time to know the family as a unity, and as the copy of a greater, an exemplary unity. Unity was respectable then. There *was* unity then. In *reality*. But now? . . .

There was unity in the family insofar as there was a head of the family. There *still* was. The paterfamilias. Such a head of the family that at one time he had the right of life and death over his own family. But now? . . . Then, little by little, the authority of the head of the family began to wane—along with, and as a reflection of, the waning of other, greater authorities. The head of the family, like the monarch, went from being an absolute head to the condition of a "constitutional" head of the family. And now that constitutional monarchs are also on the wane . . .

Don't even speak to me of a family set up as a republic.

If our epoch has a distinguishing characteristic, it is that it is full of forms that have outlived their own content. One of those forms is the family—"my" family.

I sit down at the table in the quality of head of the family. A "nominal" quality. Head of the family "on the census form." No one has taken this quality from me: I have taken it from myself. Like a suit not cut to my measure. Like a "phantasmal" suit.

What, then, is the use of this shadow of a thing that is no more? What is the use of this reflection of something that is no more? . . . Today, at my table, during the passing of the plates (passing the plates: one of the most repeated forms of "domestic madness," a sort of "alimentary roulette"), a doubt arose in our midst as to whether the plate should stop first before me, or before my daughter. With my support, the priority of my daughter prevailed—she being a woman. *Heureusement que, dans un pays si profondément antiféministe, nous sommes encore quelques-uns à soutenir les droits des femmes.*[1]

The unity of the family being dead, the "sacredness" of the family being dead, there remains the absurdity of a council of the irreconcilable. The disorder, the annoyance of a simultaneity of different rhythms, of different and often opposed ideas, of words that collide, that clash . . . Like a city street in which the traffic is not regulated, automobiles and hand carts going up and down the same side.

I'm writing these things at night, while the family sleeps, in silence and solitude: in that sacred silence, in that holy solitude which reconciles the irreconcilable.

Let us profit from this silence, from this solitude, to listen to the voice of a dead woman, of a great dead woman: Alcestis the daughter of Samuel.[2] She will speak of the relations between parents and children and their different destinies.

"Our children cannot stay with us, and should not. We ourselves cannot stay with our children, and should not. Our pace is different, our rhythm is different . . . In life, children and parents live together. But that is a mistake. An absurdity. Men, up to a certain point, walk the road of life, and living is the only purpose of their walking. Men are then children. That is why children walk and are not aware of walking—are not aware of living. That is why their time is so long. But, from that certain point on, the aim of life is no longer life, but death. We go on walking in life, but what we see in it is no longer life but death. Men are then fathers—they are parents. We then begin to be aware that we are walking—to be aware that we are living. And then we see that our way is short. And becomes ever shorter. At what precise moment does the change of course occur? . . . I do not know.

There is no precise moment. But one thing signals the shift from the road of life to the road of death: the birth of our children. In the same moment that we women bring our first child into the world—I say we women, the direct representatives of nature—the light of life ceases to shine at the end of the road before us, and instead the boundless shadow of death appears. Therefore let our children go down their own road. Down that road which we ourselves followed before they came into the world. We have nothing in common with our children. Our roads diverge. We believe we are bound to our children; our children believe they are bound to us; and there are indeed bonds, but created by ourselves, by our morality, our fantasy as parents; and by their morality, their fantasy as children. But let us not despair. One day the children will find their parents again. Will find them again in memory. Then parents and children will be reunited. Will be 'truly' reunited. When the children shift in their turn from the path whose goal is life to the path whose goal is death."

A White and Luminous House

WE HAD COME TO THIS CITY SIX months ago, my wife and I. We had stayed at the house of a friend. A colossal woman, bell-shaped, and just as resounding. A magnificent house. White, smelling of fresh paint. So many rooms and corridors we couldn't keep count of them, couldn't find the end of them. But maybe it was a circular house, and therefore infinite. Great brightness everywhere. Great possibilities of brightness, great aptitude for brightness. The same by day as by night. As I went from room to room, the walls around me awoke with light, in luminous homage. Likewise the ceiling, and the floor itself. Where was the source of this light? Besides being infinite, the house was also unfinished. Destined for prolonged construction, like the cathedrals once. From the far depths of the rooms, which I could not manage to reach, came the songs of workers and the thud of hammer blows. I cannot bear noise. Yet those songs, those same hammer blows did not disturb me. Nor, during the white nights of that house, in the white sleep I slept in that house, was I troubled by the gloomy rolling of the tram below in the street. On the contrary. That gloomy rolling wound its way into my sleep; the lullaby of a colossal nanny made of soft iron.

The staff was invisible. The head of the staff was named Leone. Not just Leone by name, Leone gracefully bore a small

37

lion's head, and, instead of speaking, emitted minuscule roars. Docile and obsequious.

A catastrophic din broke the white silence every now and then. It neither surprised nor worried me. I knew. It was our friend's child. Rosy, blond, a little angel. Children play. Our friend's son also played. Galloped, shrieking gaily, through the infinite line of rooms, halls, corridors. Took heavy metal objects in his soft hands and threw them at the windows, at the frosted glass of the doors, at the mirrors that prolonged the walls into glittering depths. Windows, frosted glass, mirrors rained down in splinters on the floor, scattering bluish sparks. But, when the smashing was over, they set about reconstituting themselves in their health and wholeness, because the impulse that moved the child's little hands was a response not to wickedness, but to an innocent need for play. In human operations, what counts is the intention.

That day I was armed with greater courage. I pushed further ahead in my exploration of the rooms. I came in sight of a little crowd. People dressed in black shirts. Bent over little anvils. Lit from above by lamps hooded by conical shades. And beating on the anvils with fine and perfectly silent little hammers.

I took a few more steps, so as to find out what this minute and precious work might be. But I bumped my nose against an invisible obstruction. A sheet of glass closed off the space between me and the little crowd of minute workers. One of them raised his eyes. They were dark, deep, inky. He looked at me but did not see me. The glass obliterated me.

If someone from the obscure world outside the white and luminous house still wrote to me, a chill creature would emerge from the depths of the shining corridors, would come to meet me silently and, by virtue of the spell alone, would stop three steps away from me, fixing on me two dark and deep beacons, which gave out not a gaze but a sort of cosmic ray, and, with the voice of a ventriloquist, would say: "A letter, Your Excellency."

"Excellency? . . ." The language of fairy tales.

We left. We left the white and luminous house. So Adam and Eve, too, must have felt on abandoning the earthly paradise. In us, moreover, there was no consciousness of sin.

The white and luminous house will go on. It will go on in my mind. Whole. In all its whiteness. In all its brightness. And I thought, I knew, that one day, amidst the silent blaring of trumpets, we would come back . . .

Months went by. We went to other cities, and from the sea to the mountains.

The day before yesterday, at last, we returned to that same city. The taxi took us as far as the intersection of two roads. And stopped there. Why? Why didn't he turn? Two stonecutters, their heads covered with newspaper caps, their flanks protected by upright matting, were chiseling away at some stone slabs by the entrance to the smaller street. Caesar's death was also preceded by signs, and Caesar ignored them. The taxi driver tried to enter the street from the other end. But it was one-way. He came back to the previous point. He stopped twenty meters from the main gateway. We had to drag the suitcase behind us. An enormous suitcase. Extremely heavy.

My wife has a suitcase complex. A suitcase is nothing but a minor form, a reduced form, of a trunk. My wife has a trunk complex. For many years I didn't understand. One day I understood.

My wife has a domestic soul. Domestic and familial. In her house, near her children, she is happy. With that superior happiness which is the repose of the soul in the midst of an assurance of affection. She had also been happy, and in the same way, in her paternal home. Then she became an actress. Traveled. Went as far as California. Her mother followed her journey in an encyclopedia printed in the middle of the last century, in which California was described as a land of outlaws and redskins who scalped the heads of travelers, and she sent letters to the Italian consular authorities appealing for protection. My wife, unable to bring the house with her in those travels, brought a trunk with her. A trunk with three partitions, three floors. A trunk that *represented* the house. *Substituted* for the house.

Today, in our travels, the simulacrum of the house accompanies her still. No longer a trunk, but a suitcase. Small for a trunk, but enormous for a suitcase. And extremely heavy. My obsession.

In the cold, in the inhospitality of hotel rooms, my wife opens the suitcase every now and then and *looks into the house*. It comforts her.

We went up three floors, dragging the suitcase behind us. What matter? We were about to reenter paradise.

It was extinguished. It was the skeleton of paradise. There had been a fire, a flood. Or some other disaster. I don't know. No more light, no more white, no more docile lion, no more chill creature with spellbinding beacons for eyes, no more child, no more windows raining down in pieces and reconstituting themselves on their own.

Silence and desolation. I was afraid to look. I also saw that old lady in mid-flight through rooms no longer white but black.

What to do? Call out to her?

No. She was shaken by choreic movements.

We went back down the stairs, dragging the simulacrum of a house behind us.

And that which remains inscribed in our minds—where is it now? What labors must be performed, what initiations gone through, to what humiliations must we be subjected, in order to find it again?

A Head Goes Flying

ARE THEY STICKING A PIG? . . . No: it's a woman's screams. I go running across the corridor, throw open the front door.

I live on the ground floor. My door opens on the landing, to the left, at the head of twelve marble steps that go down to the front gate. A nineteenth-century house. A gate made of metal bars. Fourteen centimeters between the bars. An elephant cage. My son Ruggero, when he was smaller and we came home after ten, did not wait for me to open the gate with the key: he slipped between the bars, leaped up seven steps of the marble stairway in a single bound, and pushed the button on the wall that released the lock of the gate, and the Savinio family, through the merit of its youngest member, entered the house without any trouble. This Alcinean entry did not take place on days when there was no electricity.[1]

On the same landing, opposite, live the Scachi. One morning one of the Scachi, the grandmother, burst in on us, stammered: "My daughter is dying," and collapsed on the sofa, as if she, too, were dead. My wife snatched a bottle of smelling salts and went running over there. The next day, Annibale, the doorkeeper, tied a white ribbon to the elephant cage. The eloquence of gates has only two notes. The other is the gate half closed: a sign that there has been a death in the house.

Beyond my landing, a door with windows, fan-shaped. Farther beyond, the doorkeeper's lodge with Annibale in it: a fat bird that has lost its song.

My doorkeeper is pious and has tender feet.

For several years we lived on the third floor of the same house. Going out of the house or coming back in, one had to pass by the doorkeeper. Since our descent to the ground floor, there is no longer this obligation. A profound change. I understood the effects on us of a despot's eye. When I was a child, my parents admonished me that hiding was no use: even in the most secret places, the Eye finds you. Under fascism, I again felt the Eye. Despotism infantilizes the most adult peoples.

Going out to the landing, I got into a little assembly. Two women were leaving through the gate. In a hurry. I saw them from behind. I was struck by their size—their shape. They were wearing gray *tailleurs*.[2] Identical. More than *tailleurs*, uniforms. They were carrying something between them: a woman. Very different from them. Old. Tiny. Bent. Boneless inside a white nightshirt. For a moment I saw the flash of a shiny, pink little cranium. One of the female soldiers bent down, picked up the wig, replaced it awkwardly on the old woman's head. She went on screaming like a stuck pig. All three got into an automobile parked at the curb. Or, better, the two female soldiers threw their white and quivering bundle into the automobile and climbed in after it. The automobile raced off.

In the little assembly were the Scachi in full; there was Annibale the doorkeeper, with his wife Adalgisa and his daughters Giorgina and Tomasina; Signora Miriffo and the lawyer Pirco, who also lived on the ground floor, but on the other side of the glass door; there were the tenants of the second floor, the third, the fourth. The ground floor has this additional advantage, that you have

a "summary" of the whole house. The tenants of the fifth floor
were missing—*pour cause.*

I asked the doorkeeper, "What's happened?"

"Portano via la testa." That is, "They're taking the head
away."

I pictured a head flying off, madness sweeping over the world.

My impression would have been different if Annibale had formulated his phrase differently.

Once Annibale the doorkeeper wore a brown uniform, the
chest barred with metal buttons, and a visored cap. Back then,
Annibale spoke of the tenants with deference. He said "Signor
Commendatore Pirco." He said "Her Excellency the generaless Puti di Valmescia" (the tenant of the third floor). He said
"Signora the baroness Testa di Cuvolo" (the tenant of the fifth
floor). Me he called "Signor Professore." But in my house the
rents are blocked. For several years no one has seen any longer
to replacing the doorkeeper's uniform. The latter, in winter, still
wears the overcoat with metal buttons, though it's on its last legs.
But the cap has had to be replaced by a homburg.

Since Annibale replaced the cap with a homburg, an egali-
tarian complex has formed in him. Authoritarian rulers are well
acquainted with the effects of uniforms. Annibale now no longer
says "Her Excellency the generaless Puti di Valmescia"; he says
"Puti" *tout court.* Me he no longer calls "Signor Professore."

The phrase "Portano via la testa" should therefore be inter-
preted thus: "They're taking away the baroness Testa di Cuvolo."
But why were they? And who were those two broad-shouldered
and militaryish women?

"Two nurses from the asylum for the criminally insane.
They've taken the baroness away because she's a murderer."

So said Adalgisa, wife of Annibale the doorkeeper. Adalgisa

usually spoke in a clipped and rudimentary fashion. But in telling me the dreadful story of the baroness Testa di Cuvolo, Adalgisa used the most exact words, the most well-formed periods. A clear confirmation that one speaks well (and writes well) when one has something to say. And the story of the baroness Testa di Cuvolo gives one much to say.

The baroness Emma Testa di Cuvolo was a widow. She had a son, Riccardo, now going on thirty-six. She had also had a daughter, Linda, who had died of typhus at the age of seven, while the baroness was pregnant with Riccardo. When Riccardo came into the world, Emma united in her son her love for her dead daughter as well. Riccardo became a double creature: man and woman, a complete creature. Being a widow, Emma brought up her son by herself. Absolutely and extremely jealous. She began to tour Europe, bringing with her, like an appendix, this melancholy, obedient boy.

Riccardo turned thirty. Wrote a little. Painted a little. With poetic fantasy, singular, profound. Riccardo's works never crossed the threshold of the house. The mother alone read, saw, appreciated, understood. *E basta.* Riccardo himself was content, desired nothing else. Riccardo was the greatest writer in the world, the greatest painter in the world. Both were convinced, deeply. Riccardo's artistic independence was assured by a solid capital left by Riccardo's father, of which mother and son regularly consumed the fruits.

Riccardo rarely went out alone. But once was enough. He met a girl, he fell in love with her, and since Riccardo did everything seriously, he married the girl, married her in secret from his mother. When the baroness learned (indirectly) that "her" Riccardo had taken a wife, it was the end of the world. Did that simpleton have any need of a wife? Wasn't his mother enough for him? Riccardo was chased out of the house.

For three months, Riccardo and his wife lived as vagrants. But those were three months of torture for the baroness Emma. Only so as to have her Riccardo back, she took in the intruder as well. It was life in hell: a frozen hell. The baroness ignored the son's wife. She looked right through her. As if her daughter-in-law were transparent. As if she weren't there. At moments, walking, she would bump into her.

Then, all at once, the situation changed. The baroness "discovered" Anna. Became fond of her. Loved her. More and more. Made her presents of her jewelry. All of it. Put it on her. Herself. Covered her with necklaces, earrings, bracelets. Took her to the dressmakers. Ordered clothes for her by her own fantasy, gaudy and old-fashioned. Took her to plays, receptions, balls, while Riccardo, alone in the house, went on writing, painting. She was glad when men paid suit to Anna. She encouraged the suitors. *She was seeking a husband for her daughter-in-law.* In Anna she had recovered Linda, her little girl who had died of typhus at the age of seven.

Riccardo, in his silence, was aware of it all. In spirit he was inclined to happy solutions. His mother was seeking a husband for Anna? One day she would become aware that there was a husband—himself—and the "problem" would be solved in the simulacrum of a new marriage, different from the first, tragic one: reconciled, happy.

Riccardo, in his silence, awaited the solution. And perhaps the solution would have come. But one night, in the dark, Anna, by half hints, made Riccardo to understand that in her there was something changed—something certain.

When the baroness Emma, much later, also came to know Anna's changed condition, horror fell upon the house of Testa. Riccardo was her son, Anna her daughter. Riccardo and Anna were brother and sister. And now . . .

One morning, Annibale the doorkeeper once again tied a white ribbon to the bars of the elephant cage.

At night the baroness Emma went into her son's studio. Riccardo was sleeping on the sofa bed. He woke up with a start before this aged specter. The aged specter said: "I haven't forgotten that you're my son. Despite all the harm you've done me. No matter. You needn't worry about it any more. *I've put things in order.*"

Adalgisa, in the end, made this comment, revealing a profound logic. She said: "If a grandmother is a mother twice over, a grandmother who strangles her little grandchild in the cradle is an infanticide twice over."

The assembly of tenants broke up. The elevator was closed for servicing. We climbed on foot to the fifth floor. We stopped outside the baroness' door. There was nothing to be heard.

We went down again. A head went flying before me.

Orpheus the Dentist

I HAD DECIDED TO LEAVE ON TUESDAY. But starting Saturday, when, in the evening, I had the supreme joy of hearing a broadcast of my radio opera *Agenzia Fix* on the radio,[1] a dull pain began to occupy, at ever more frequent intervals, the upper right side of my jaw, and to spread itself through my head, like a spider its legs.

I thought: "It's him." *He* was one of my last premolars. He had already made himself felt at other times. The pain would wake up, torment me for several days, doze off again; sometimes for whole seasons, like snakes.

Teeth are cunning. His predecessors had done the same. Until, one by one, they left. Without remorse. Yet teeth are part of us. And, in some men, a very important, very "functional" part. In Woodrow Wilson, for example; in Franklin Delano Roosevelt. Yet, despite the extremely important function that teeth have had in the mouths of these two presidents of the United States, many citizens of those States have their teeth pulled, in full youth and perfect conditions of dental health, and replace them with false teeth.

Why say false? Better to say painless. At the end of this May, the Piccolo Teatro di Milano will produce a work of mine, *The Alcestis of Samuel*. The one who will bring Alcestis back from Hades this time is not Hercules but Franklin Delano Roosevelt. By no means an arbitrary substitution. Perfectly justified. As I

47

myself explain in the context, and as the audience will certainly understand, Hercules is not a singular figure, confined to the son of Alcmene. Hercules, that "purgator," is a figure who periodically renews himself. The penultimate Hercules, in order of time, was Giuseppe Garibaldi; the latest was Franklin Delano Roosevelt. In my version of Alcestis, the part of Hercules, that is, of Roosevelt, will be played by Camillo Piloto. Piloto, at the present time, is studying the physiognomy of the President in minute particulars on photographic documents in the American Library of Rome: the form of the eyeglasses, which did not hook over the ears like mine or yours, but were pinched to the nose; and meanwhile a brave dental technician is fabricating a row of enormous teeth which, in the actor's mouth, will imitate the famous laugh.

In 1914, in Paris, I got to know a citizen of the United States, of Mexican origin: Marius de Zayas. He had a pair of Nietzschean mustaches which, starting from under his nostrils, fell in a hairy cascade over his sharp and obstinate chin. Marius de Zayas was a theater impresario. In July 1914, he made an agreement with Apollinaire and me for a tour of lectures and concerts the following autumn to several cities of the United States, during which Apollinaire's *Breasts of Tiresias* would be staged, accompanied by music written for the occasion by me.[2] A month later the First World War broke out.

The mustaches of Marius de Zayas had not only an ornamental function but also hid his mouth, empty and black as a cave. Zayas, though he was going on thirty then and was immune to cavities, had spent some time in a clinic in New York, and had all thirty-two of his teeth removed one after the other; but, unable to bear dentures, which he abandoned in the water glasses of hotel rooms during his frequent travels, he chewed every sort of food, down to the toughest steak, with his bare gums.

In contrast to Marius de Zayas, toothless and a most robust chewer, we may cite the god Pushan, an Indian colleague of the Greek Hermes and the Latin Mercury, because Pushan, like the son of Zeus and Maia, was also a god of the roads, and not only guided men on their earthly roads, but continued to guide them on the roads of the beyond. Pushan performed his functions as a guide seated on a little cart drawn by goats, and although, unlike Zayas, his gums were armed with leonine teeth, he ate only foods soaked in water.

Two years ago I visited the convent of Saint Francis in Paola. The saint's relics are kept in a glass case in the church. While Francis was living and working as a saint in Calabria, Louis XI, in France, was casually killing off, by means of other hands, all those who somehow got in his way, and killed so many that in the end, despite a very tough conscience, he began to feel the sting of remorse. How to heal it? The king was told that an Italian monk by the name of Francis, who lived in far-off Calabria, was a good healer of consciences, and Louis ordered that the healer come to France without delay, as today, for the same reason, they call in some famous psychoanalyst: for example, the father of that young American student who, not long ago, married the sister of the Shah of Persia, in a civil ceremony in Civitavecchia, and is now studying the Koran so as to be able to marry her religiously as well. Francis had a sister. Seeing him on the point of departure, she said to him: "You're going so far, and you're not leaving me anything to remember you by?" "Yes, I'm leaving you something," replied Francis, and, so saying, he pulled out a canine tooth with two fingers and left it to his sister to remember him by. Extremely white, this canine tooth now gleams in the glass case of relics, in the church of Saint Francis in Paola. On the relations between Louis XI and Saint Francis of Paola, Casimir Delavigne wrote, as is known, a ridiculous play.[3]

So I thought: "It's him." And I thought: "Until he quiets down, it's not prudent for me to go traveling." And that morning, instead of making my way to the station, I made my way to my dentist.

My dentist is not only an excellent odontologist; he is also a man of culture and a first-rate musician. Two years ago, at his invitation, I took myself to his house one afternoon, this time to sit not in the articulated mechanical chair in his dental office, but on a more peaceful one in his drawing room, and hear a short but pithy concert: a sonata for cello and piano by Shostakovich, some lyrics by Mahler, and a very tender *Ave Maria* from the hand of the master of the house, which a Spanish baritone, brown as a young bull from Triana, the school of bullfighters, sang with a velvet voice.

But my dentist is not only an excellent odontologist, and a man of culture, and a musician; he is also a kindly soul. I'll say more: he is Orpheus. His sure hand had just finished extracting "Him" from his socket, my right cheek was numb and prickly from the effects of Novocain (the strange condition of hemiplegics, who drag half of themselves behind them, reduced to a phantasm), and he invited me to go to the drawing room with him. Sitting on the bench of his Hammond organ, still in his white coat, he pulled out a few stops, pressed on a pedal, placed his right hand on the upper keyboard, which is that of the melody, and his left on the lower one, which is that of the accompaniment, and played a Lullaby of his own composition and of an infinite tenderness; and the hateful memory of "Him" gradually vanished into the harmonious heaven of Euterpe.

I, Daphne

FROM ROME, WHERE I LIVE, I OFTEN go to Milan, where I work. In Milan I have no house. Hence I take my meals and my repose in a café in the center which is at the same time a restaurant and a meeting-place. There is in this café and restaurant a cloakroom girl. She is very nice. Her eye is ringed by a halo of shadow and rests on a plump little cushion.

Besides which, as cloakroom girl and at the same time guardian of the most intimate places, she has that helpful and at the same time neutral air that midwives and nurses have. I am on the threshold of old age, but owing to my peculiar disposition, old age is mingled in me with as much infantility; not to be confused—may my friends forgive me—with what commonly goes under the name of second childhood; hence I now feel more need of assistance than when I was a child.

Many times over the course of the past winter I came to Milan. In the winter I usually wear an overcoat. And, dropping by my usual café three, or four, or even five or six times a day, before sitting at a table in the café or restaurant, I would go to deposit my overcoat in the cloakroom; and the cloakroom girl with the shaded and plump eye would take it from my back as if, like Saint Bartholomew, I were surrendering my covering of skin to her and was left in my bare muscles. Then, before leaving, I would return to the cloakroom, and the cloakroom girl with the shaded and plump eye would hold my skin out to me like a cross, which I, with my back to her, would slip on, with that studied haste, with that violated shame of someone being helped into his underwear.

Thus there were established between me and the cloakroom girl with the shaded and plump eye relations from which one would not venture to say that all tenderness was excluded. And I would put in the cloakroom girl's hand each time that which the French and Germans call, with the same meaning, *pourboire* and *Trinkgeld*, and we, more vulgarly, a tip. But so much good had entered into the relations between me and the cloakroom girl that, already at the second donning of the coat in the same day, she would not want to accept the *Trinkgeld*, saying that I "had already given it to her the first time." I would insist on giving it, she on refusing it; we arrived at a plastic, mimetic, choreographic form, at a ballet of giving and refusing. All we lacked was the music.

One day I went running out, having deposited the *Trinkgeld* on the cloakroom table; the cloakroom girl ran after me, trying to stuff the *Trinkgeld* back into my coat pocket.

Thus between us a little myth was born. The myth of Daphne and Apollo was reborn between us; in which version the roles were reversed, Apollo being the cloakroom girl and I Daphne.

However, I did not turn into a laurel. Something worse happened. I returned to Milan a few days ago. There was no more rain, nor mist (*bruma* in Italian; the beautiful word *brumista*, the Milanese cabbie, has unfortunately fallen into disuse by force of circumstances), nor cold. A magnificent sun and a soft warmth in the air.

I went into my usual café and restaurant and sat at a table. But bare of my overcoat. The cloakroom girl was standing on the threshold of the cloakroom. There were scarcely ten meters between us. Her glance carried much further. But this time Apollo did not run after Daphne, did not try to seize her: did not even look at her. Thus a change of season destroys a myth.

Can I deny a certain disappointment?

There are similar disappointments in clinics and hospitals. Freshly operated on, the sisters and nurses treated me like a fragile newborn. What care! What affection! There was nothing more precious than my health. As I recovered, the care waned; the solicitude waned; the affection of the sisters and nurses waned. No longer a fragile newborn: I was a solid adult.

I left the clinic amidst general indifference.

Is it bad to get better?

Solitude

EACH MORNING SIGNOR DIDO BEGINS the day by reading the newspaper. That is the first invasion that Signor Dido suffers. It would be easy for Signor Dido to fend off this invasion. He could simply not read the newspaper. But how can one renounce renewing one's contact with the world each morning? Emerging from the fiction of dreams, Signor Dido feels the need to reenter reality. But are dreams really fiction? And is reality truly real?

Signor Dido looks at the newspaper each morning to find out the situation of the world, and whether some new fact, propitious or unpropitious, has intervened in it; but he looks at it above all in search of some thread of sympathy to which he could tie his own threads of sympathy.

Charles Darwin studied the relations between the individual and the environment, but he didn't know a thing about psychology. He therefore did not notice that at the basis of the relations between the individual and the environment is the need for sympathy, even more necessary than the right temperature for our bodies. Signor Dido searches each morning for that necessary thread of sympathy. To help him live.

Vain search. Which becomes still more vain when Signor Dido goes on from news of a political, warlike, economic, or reportorial character to news of an intellectual character. Whose fault is it: his or the intellectuals'?

Even wars have lost their one-time frankness: either wholly sympathetic or wholly antipathetic. Today wars have an ambiguous character. Like everything today. That is, moreover, the misfortune of our time: not being able to opt fully for this or that principle, or for this or that man, or for this or that thing. The misfortune of our time, or the "private" misfortune of Signor Dido?

Having reached the bottom of the last page, and having found no trace of that sympathy he was searching for; forced, on the contrary, to drive back the columns of antipathy assaulting him from every side, Signor Dido withdraws into himself. He is a skein of which the tip of the thread hangs exhausted, hopeless.

Then Signor Dido's "personal" day begins. The passage from the general world to the personal world is neither easy nor quick. Signor Dido cleans himself up. As if scraping from his back one by one the spatters which, on a rainy day, in a muddy street, an automobile had splashed on him passing by at high speed.

Meanwhile Signor Dido looks out the window. The contemplation of nature, according to ancient opinion, placates anguish and comforts the soul. Beyond the window, Signor Dido's eye encounters as much of nature as the city allows: the trees lining the avenue, a corner of sky.

The house opposite is a colossal segment of concrete, which, like a wedge, meets Signor Dido's gaze with its acute angle. In the windows of the fifth floor the sun sparkles. On a little third-floor balcony, a young housemaid is vigorously beating a carpet. A crested and spherical nanny goes down the sidewalk pushing a baby carriage. Clouds trace a white alphabet in the sky.

Nature, like this, from a distance, has a calm—perhaps

noble—aspect. But nature is also neutral; that there is no concealing. And neutralism is not what Signor Dido needs; he needs sympathy. What new disappointments would Signor Dido have, if he could hear close by, and in their own voices, in their own language, what such clear air, such a pure sky, such white clouds are saying and thinking? Maybe worse than those caused him by the words of men, the thoughts of men transcribed in the newspapers.

Little by little, Signor Dido manages to rid himself of foreign elements. He finally comes back to being *all himself*. Happiness begins. *His* happiness. The purest happiness. The only happiness.

But here the doorbell rings. They bring him the mail. Anticipation and hope. Hope for the unexpected. The thread of sympathy may come in an envelope.

No: two letters full of insults. Readers who have recently read something written by Signor Dido—and the moment has come to say it: Signor Dido is a writer by profession—and reacted like snakes whose tails have been stepped on. In one a curse is even accurately formulated! The third letter is addressed to Comm. Cencetti, the tenant on the third floor, and has been brought to Signor Dido by mistake. Of the payment that Signor Dido has been awaiting with increasing impatience for so many days, there is not the slightest trace.

An athlete in the struggle against disappointments, Signor Dido manages even this time to drive out of himself the effect of the two insulting letters, and reenters the ineffable sphere of his own happiness.

He writes. He takes wing again. Without leaps. Without jolts. In "his" sky.

But here he is standing up. A stimulus from the diencephalon, the hunger center, tears him from the desk, propels him down the corridor, carries him to the credenza, in which, usually, there lies, blackened, shriveled, some remnant of the evening meal: a scrap of prosciutto, a bit of cheese.

This morning the credenza is filled as always with plates, crockery, table linen, but empty of alimentary substances. Something catches Signor Dido's eye in the semi-darkness. On top of a white stack of plates. Hope is kindled in Signor Dido's soul. He reaches out a hand: it is a folded napkin trimmed with lace. But here is the soup tureen. In this tureen Signora Dido sometimes hides away a bit of parmesan. Destined to be grated and then sprinkled over the pasta or the broth. In this gesture of Signora Dido's lies the "wisdom" of the mistress of the house; the accommodating intention of removing the surplus food from the devouring lusts of Signor Dido and hiding it away, without openly putting it under lock and key. Uncovered, the tureen proves to be as white, and smooth, and clean inside as it is white, and smooth, and clean outside.

And this other tureen? The credenza has two levels. On the lower level, Signor Dido makes out a tureen he doesn't know. A pink tureen. He reaches out a hand: it is the crown of one of his wife's hats. A straw hat. Pink.

Signor Dido slowly returns to his desk. Weighed down with an additional disappointment. Because the stimulus that propelled him to the credenza was not only hunger: it was also the need for sympathy; above all the need for sympathy. In brutes, eating is an act surrounded by darkness. In men like Signor Dido, eating is also a making ours, out of sympathy, of something we take from outside: meat, greens, milk products, fruit—nature. For Signor Dido, eating is an act of love.

In the afternoon, the vain search for sympathy becomes even more burdensome. It is six o'clock. The blinds are closed, the lights turned on: a barrier is placed between domestic life and the life of the city, of the world. The warm and gentle triumph of the family.

Signor Dido's daughter bursts into her papa's studio. Followed by young Silvio. Both excited. Trembling. Overflowing with things to say. They have come back from seeing a documentary on Burma. What a marvelous country! What temples! What sacred dances! . . . Signor Dido takes it. Puts up with it. He who has always had an insuperable aversion for the exotic, and now more than ever.

Signor Dido slips on his overcoat, goes out. The day before they had called him to come and hear some recorded music. Extraordinary!

He goes.

The drawing room is in semi-darkness, dotted with low lights, similar to flowers but more flimsy than flowers. Three men and two women, seated at some distance from one another, incline their heads, absorbed in contrapuntal harmonies. A radio-gramophone reels off the Brandenburg Concertos one after the other. Between concerto and concerto it emits a raucous gurgling, as if, having gulped down the piece of music, it were now digesting it.

Many of Signor Dido's contemporaries, horrified by the "dispersion" of our time, take refuge in pre-Beethovenian music, as in a safe oasis. So architectonic! So devoid of doubts! So serene! Not Signor Dido. A profoundly romantic soul, Signor Dido not only does not shun dispersion, but loves it. He prefers being carried by this tempestuous and infinite sea to putting in at any port. Only even in this sweet and desperate shipwreck he would like sympathy, and to drag with him all men, all women: all humanity: all the universe.

The day is over. Signor Dido's body is stretched out in bed. His bald head rests on the pillow. His hand, which has just abandoned Concetto Marchesi's lucid history of Latin literature, will go up to the switch of the lamp. And Signor Dido will reenter his dreams.

Is this the sympathy he was seeking?

No. Even dreams are foreign to him. "Our" dreams. And antipathetic. Except for one. That dream of "himself" that Signor Dido would like to dream and always re-dream. That dream of himself into which all things enter, and blend, and become himself.

Diké

A FEW YEARS AGO, SIGNORA DIDO took into her service a house-keeper: Rosa Profumo.

In the Dido household, as in many other households besides, servant crises are renewed every six months, like the equinoxes. Of each new housekeeper that Signora Dido takes into her service, she says to Signor Dido: "This time we've done it. A pearl. Look at the kitchen! What order! What cleanliness! . . . Whereas that sloven . . . Greasy fingers. I didn't say anything to you, because men don't understand certain things. It takes patience like mine."

At the end of a week, Signora Dido, returning to the conversation about the new housekeeper, confided to Signor Dido: "She's grown fond of me. Even too much so. This one, you'll see, even cannon fire won't make her leave."

Signor Dido thought: "It's not we who send these housekeepers away: it's they who suddenly show an unrestrainable need to quit our house." But Signor Dido kept this thought to himself.

Several peaceful months followed, until, at the approach of the new equinox, ever more excited dialogues between Signora Dido and the housekeeper began to reach Signor Dido's ears, through the door to the studio, and the corridor, and the door to the kitchen. Signor Dido thought: "The crisis has begun."

At the table, hedging his words with caution, Signor Dido tried to find out the cause of the changed relations between Signora Dido and the housekeeper, but in vain. Signora Dido, after much rambling, replied: "Better not to speak of it." And she gulped down mouthfuls with such force as if she were swallowing not alimentary substances softened by cooking, but stones.

Signor Dido ended by thinking that, after several months of continuous relations with the same housekeeper, a sort of psychic poisoning developed in Signora Dido, which she could be cured of only by sending the housekeeper away. The same thing, moreover, also happens between friends, between married couples, between lovers. One day perhaps chemistry will clarify this form of poisoning by cohabitation. The Greeks say *paragnoristikamai*: "We have overknown each other."

The arrival of Rosa Profumo signaled a new era in the Dido household. Months went by, the cape of the first year was rounded, and Signora Dido went on saying that in the person of Rosa Profumo she had found the pearl of housekeepers.

Rosa Profumo was not only the pearl of housekeepers, but she was also young and beautiful. She pleased the friends of the Dido household, almost all intellectuals. She especially pleased a friend of Signor Dido's, a teacher of experimental psychology who, being at dinner one evening in the Dido household together with his own wife, found a way of passing a note to Rosa Profumo, arranging a meeting for the next day in a tearoom.

Autumn came; winter was at the door. One morning Signora Dido came into Signor Dido's studio and with an unusually gentle voice said to him: "Poor thing, she wants a fur coat! . . . She's found one, of blond lambskin, at a good price, and payable in installments; but they say her signature isn't enough: they also want yours."

The next day an austere gentleman in a dark suit presented himself in the Dido household, a leather briefcase in his hand. He did not want to confide in Signora Dido and said he had to speak with Signor Dido in person.

Shown into the studio and the door closed behind him, the austere gentleman proved affable and sympathetic. The "commendatore" wished to give a blond lambskin coat to Signorina Rosa Profumo? A magnificent "item." And such a beautiful girl . . .

Signor Dido signed the promissory note.

Winter passed. Rosa Profumo, in a coat of blond lambskin, was seen in the most expensive cinemas and in the most elegant tearooms, accompanied by the teacher of experimental psychology, the friend of the Dido household. Spring came.

Spring came and one day Signor and Signora Dido left for a city in northern Italy. They came back after a month. Signor Dido opened the door with his key. There was no Rosa Profumo; the house had been ransacked.

Signor and Signora Dido found enormous bills from the butcher, the grocer, the other retailers of the quarter. Besides that, Rosa Profumo, abusing the name of Signora Dido, had taken whole lengths of fabric on credit from Signor Ciccio, the tobacconist, who, along with selling salts and tobaccos, also ran a little emporium. The promissory notes he had signed himself for the acquisition by installments of the blond lambskin coat came back to Signor Dido, rejected.

Great was the pain of Signora Dido; still greater was her surprise. Rosa! A thief! Who would have thought it?

Signora Dido telephoned a lawyer who was a friend of the house: she asked him to proceed against a certain Profumo Rosa through legal channels. Profumo Rosa was accused before the judicial authorities; the accusation was committed to the District

Court. Signora Dido received a summons hand delivered by the court clerk to present herself at the District Court on such and such a day, at such and such an hour.

Signora Dido presented herself at the District Court, waited a long time in an extremely unpleasant place and among extremely unpleasant people, and was finally informed by a very skinny little old man, poorly dressed and manifestly atrabilious, that the case had been adjourned.

Why? . . . A mystery.

The promissory notes had meanwhile been paid by Signor Dido, and so had the debts to the retailers. The rancor in Signora Dido's soul died down. She telephoned the lawyer who was a friend of the house and asked him to withdraw the accusation.

Three months passed. Signora Dido received a summons hand delivered by the court clerk to present herself at the District Court on such and such a day, at such and such an hour.

How so? The accusation had been withdrawn . . .

Years passed. Every three months, Signora Dido received a summons hand delivered by the court clerk to present herself at the District Court on such and such a day, at such and such an hour.

Caught in the august net of Justice, Signora Dido, no longer knowing where to turn, turned to Signor Dido.

"What are we to do?"

"Diké," replied Signor Dido, "is universal Justice. According to Orpheus, she sits beside the throne of Zeus, from where she watches over the actions of mortals. Diké protects the innocent and punishes the guilty. But the sense of justice is so profound in Justice that the protection she gives to the innocent is no less severe than the punishment she gives to the guilty."

"What are we to do?" Signora Dido asked again.

"Nothing," replied Signor Dido. "Nothing. Diké is venerable and inexorable. And what's more, she's blind."

"Enough!" cried Signora Dido. "One can't talk with you!"

The front doorbell. "Signora Dido Anna Maria? . . . A summons to present yourself . . ."

The Bearded Gentleman

IT HAPPENED ON THE EVENING OF December 31, in the Dido household. And the Dido family was puffed up with pride: Signora Marta, Signorina Marfisa, twenty-two years old, and even Signor Dido himself a little.

The young Rinaldo Dido, a senior in high school and the protagonist of the event we are about to narrate, was also puffed up with pride. Less puffed up, however, than the deuteragonists, that is, his parents and sister. Soldiers on the field rejoice less at a battle won than combatants on the internal front, in their armchairs and with newspapers in their hands.

We will add that the pride which swelled the breast of the Dido family on the evening of December 31, and which today, more than a month later, has still not ceased to swell it, was felt but unspoken. Except by Signor Dido the father, who not only did not keep silent about this feeling, but commented on it. Because in the bosom of his own family, Signor Dido sometimes played the part of the devil's advocate.

It was the vacation at year's end. On the morning of December 31, young Rinaldo Dido, together with a friend of his, set out at an early hour for the Terminillo.

His mother had outfitted him thoroughly: hobnailed boots, thick gloves, a knitted cap that came down over the ears.

Young Rinaldo left, and that same evening, at around eight, he reappeared on the threshold of the paternal home, supported by the friend, and his leg dangling.

A skiing fracture.

The Dido family was puffed up with pride.

• • •

It had happened like this. The ski had sunk into the soft snow, and, in sinking, had bent edgewise, compelling the foot which was fastened to the ski to bend as well, and then the leg which is the continuation of the foot. "A classic skiing fracture," the orthopedist diagnosed after a summary examination, as a man much experienced in this sort of fracture, so frequent in our era of winter sports.

The x-ray confirmed the fracture of that outer bone of the leg which everyone calls the fibyoola, and which is properly called the fiboola.

The orthopedist came back the next day, dressed in a white coat, and set the limb in plaster. He was assisted by a Herculean orderly in a leather jacket, who left a big red motorcycle lying on its side in the entryway of the Didos' house.

The young man spent two days in bed. On the third day, he slipped his trousers over the white statue's leg, and, on his own, slowly made his way to the family table.

The members of the Dido family, silent and happy, had their heads bent over the evening soup.

• • •

Each time someone happened to tell him that a young boy or girl had broken a leg or an arm while practicing the sport of skiing, Signor Dido rejoiced.

A natural joy.

Signor Dido did not belong to the winter sport generation.

At the time when he himself was young, there were as yet no

winter vacations: there were only summer vacations.

You left for the country in a carriage, on the example of Signor Quintiliano and his four sons: Ernesto, Gigetto, Adolfo, and Arturino, known as Little Shrimp.[1]

Country life, in those days, was slower, more limited. Instead of the not yet invented instruments for abbreviating time and space, there was fantasy. And when you returned to the city, the memory of the village summer stayed with you like the memory of paradise lost.

The fracture suffered on the Terminillo by his own son awakened in Signor Dido's heart that malicious but natural reaction of joy. And Signor Dido had the effrontery to show it. At the table. Amidst the exultant silence of the family.

But no one paid any attention to him.

• • •

Signora Dido looked at her son with grave eyes. Like a hero. Looked at him with new eyes.

She said:

"What a mustache you've grown yourself, Rinaldo! What sideburns!"

Indeed, a brown downiness shaded the boy's upper lip and descended over his cheeks.

Signor Dido, to whom it seemed unbelievable that the malicious words just spoken had been ignored, said:

"We'll soon be buying him a Gillette."

Signora Dido's face blazed.

"Not for anything do I wish your son also to shave his beard with a Gillette, as you've done all your life. We will buy Rinaldo an electric razor."

For Signor Dido, the outburst of Signora Dido was an unexpected success. He had not been thinking, at that moment, that a generation also distinguishes itself from the previous generation by the different instruments it uses to remove the hair on its face. But under the impression of the words spoken with such indignation by Signora Dido, Signor Dido recalled that when, forty years ago, he had bought himself a safety razor and begun shaving his beard with this new instrument, he himself had looked with disdain upon those retrogrades who went on shaving their beards with a straight razor.

While these memories were coming back to Signor Dido's head, the door to the dining room slowly opened, and a tall, extremely pale, and bearded gentleman appeared on the threshold.

Signor Dido's father, whom Signor Dido had not seen for more than forty years.

The tall, bearded gentleman smiled, and with an extremely thin hand pointed to the beard that encircled his face.

But he did not speak.

Because the dead do not speak.

The Children Speak Softly

THE DIDO FAMILY IS AT THE TABLE: Signor Dido, Signora Dido, and their two children, twenty-year-old Armida and sixteen-year-old Rinaldo. In the Dido household they are not very talkative; nevertheless, a few words pass now and then from plate to plate. Signora Dido asks young Rinaldo how things went at school today. Young Rinaldo replies in such a low voice that Signora Dido does not understand his reply. The Didos' friends praise the Didos because their two children speak softly, unlike so many Italians who do not so much speak as bombard each other. "How well you've brought up your children," say the Didos' friends. Signor Dido accepts the praise and is pleased that, unlike so many Italians who do not so much speak as fire off mortars, his children speak softly; but this speaking so softly as to render incomprehensible the few replies that Armida and Rinaldo make to the few questions of their parents arouses Signor Dido's curiosity. And Signor Dido discovers that Armida and Rinaldo speak so softly *so that their parents will not understand them.* Signor Dido discovers that this speaking so softly is a barrier between generations. Signor Dido notices that even among their friends, if the parents are present, Armida and Rinaldo speak softly, but their friends understand them. And therefore this speaking softly is also a secret speaking: a speaking among prisoners. Why?

71

The Small Plate

FOR SOME TIME NOW, SIGNOR DIDO has been restricted to a special diet for reasons of health.

At the table, during mealtimes, the food destined for Signor Dido's wife and children arrives on a big plate; the food destined for Signor Dido arrives on a small plate.

The big plate and the small plate are both brought to the table by Trebisonda, the Dido household's maid of all work.

Trebisonda is a native of a little country town in the Abruzzi.

Rural populations, unlike city populations, believe in the magic of names. They think that one's name influences one's destiny, and thus they choose the names they give to their children with great care. What hopes was the father of the maid of all work in the Dido household nursing when he fixed upon his daughter the name of Trebisonda?

Trebisonda venerates her parents. She venerates them for different reasons. In her father she venerates the man of intellect; in her mother she venerates the *univira*.[1]

In her mother Trebisonda also admires the mature beauty.

One day Trebisonda said to Signora Dido:

"My mother is still very beautiful. And she's already going on forty."

In Trebisonda's opinion, forty is very old.

Trebisonda added:

"My mother has splendid teeth. She's only missing one: in front. From an accident."

"A fall?" asked Signora Dido.

"No," replied Trebisonda. "My father knocked her down one day with a backhand."

Trebisonda actually said, not "a backhand" but "a smack in the kisser."

Trebisonda's father was famous locally as an extemporaneous poet. Poets, as we know, are subject to furor.

Trebisonda is furnished with a limited intelligence. She mangles the names she hears on the telephone; she is incapable of understanding the simplest conversation. Her voice, to make up for it, is confident and persuasive. The absurd, on her lips, acquires the ring of truth.

After Trebisonda has spoken, you think: "Why, yes. That's true." It is only on second thought that the veil is rent and the absurdity appears.

Trebisonda's conversation gives the impression of a dream.

Signor Dido is taciturn by nature. At the table even more so than away from the table. Sitting before his own small plate, glancing fleetingly at the big plate destined for his wife and children, Signor Dido keeps silent. Keeps silent and thinks. Thinks and remembers.

Remembers times long past. How old was Signor Dido back then? Two . . . Two and a half. Not more. Then, too, he sat at the family table and had special food before him. More tender.

It is the suspicion of having fallen back into infancy that humiliates Signor Dido.

No. With regard to intellectual faculties, Signor Dido is still perfectly sound.

From the point of view of alimentary quality, Signor Dido should be content. The food served to him separately on the small plate is of better quality than the food served on the big plate. Signora Dido points it out to him: "See? We're having cutlets, but I've had you served the filet." And Signora Dido bears down on her cutlet, which resists the knife.

This privileged condition does not please Signor Dido. On the contrary: it adds to his humiliation.

Trebisonda, for her part, senses and appreciates the reason why Signor Dido is served special food and of better quality. In Trebisonda's mind there speaks a most ancient patriarchalism.

Trebisonda knows that the man of the house is to be served first and best. The big plate she places unceremoniously in the middle of the table. The small plate she places before Signor Dido with a ritual slowness.

Signor Dido stares at the blank wall before him.

Why does this special alimentary treatment humiliate Signor Dido?

Perhaps because it betrays a condition of infirmity.

The man of healthy psyche feels the condition of infirmity as a shameful condition.

Signor Dido had to follow a treatment by hypodermic injections. His doctor himself came to give him the first injection.

"Lie down," said the doctor.

Signor Dido did not obey. He found such persuasive words that the doctor stuck the needle into Signor Dido's back, as with one who accepts death, but standing up.

Even metaphorically, dropping one's pants is a gesture of surrender.

Signor Dido adopted the pose of Phryne.[2]

A nurse came to give the succeeding injections. She was fat and was called Italia. After the third injection, Signor Dido took the syringe with the needle grafted to its tip and stuck it ten times into the pillow of the bed; the eleventh time he stuck it into his own flesh.

The aponia of this little operation astonished him. He was proud of himself. From that day on Signor Dido did his hypodermic injections himself, and thought that one day he would succeed in giving himself the intravenous ones as well.

The humiliating effect of the special food as the betrayal of an infirm condition does not fully convince Signor Dido.

There must be some other reason.

More remote.

What is it?

And here, at a stroke, comes the illumination.

Signor Dido has found it.

The common meal has a most ancient sacred significance. To consume the same food is to tighten the bond that unites us to the same god. Excluded from the food on the big plate, Signor Dido feels like the one who had no right to enter the temple and had to stand alone in the narthex.

Signor Dido's children seemed not to have heard him.

Signora Dido listened, but without raising her eyes from the stubborn cutlet.

In her turn she uttered a few words. She uttered them softly and with her usual intonation, which is sweet.

The words uttered by Signora Dido did not confirm Signor Dido's words, nor did they deny them. They cancelled them.

Signora Dido is defenseless against arguments and at the same time proud. She does not dispute the arguments of others; she cancels them. With sweetness. An ineffable net surrounds Signora Dido, against which the arguments of others bounce off and fall down.

Battleships were once protected against torpedoes by a net of steel.

Rage throbs in Signor Dido's temples. It is about to burst from his eyes.

Trebisonda comes in and with a ritual gesture places the small plate before Signor Dido.

Signor Dido stares at the wall.

Berenice

THE CLOCK ON THE WRITING DESK strikes once in the dark.

One AM.

Signor Dido is lying on his back in bed, his arms spread wide.

It is an old family clock. Signor Dido's mother carried it with her even when she traveled. Inside her valise, on the luggage rack of the compartment, the clock went on striking the hours, the half hours. The passengers glanced at one another.

As a young man, Signor Dido went to sleep in the position of a boxer in defense.

Defense against death?

Now that he is verging on sixty, Signor Dido no longer defends himself: he lets himself go.

A light wind stirs the window curtains. The voices of passersby rise from the street, the rapid breath of an automobile, the thin question of a child:

"Papa, is it true that . . ."

Children out at this hour?

Signor Dido keeps the door of his memories shut. Memories are dangerous. They bring shame and remorse with them.

Signor Dido opens it very rarely. And only to some light memory.

Will he open it tonight to the memory of Mary?

Mary comes in. Signor Dido's room brightens.

The faculty of brightening was Mary's most conspicuous quality. It had made her famous.

Signor Dido was living in Paris.

The air of Paris is subtle. An agile man who in Rome is able to jump a meter and a half, in Paris is able to jump two meters without any effort.

We are speaking of figurative jumping. The champions are named Voltaire, Stendhal . . .

The light that came from under Mary's skin, from within her hair, from within her eyes, from between her lips, from within her smile, which was in her voice, was more than the most admirable of natural things: it was an unnatural thing, like a dog that suddenly starts singing soprano.

With the existence of Mary—a definite, indubitable existence—there competed above all the function of justifying certain episodes in classical mythology: the Milky Way, Berenice's hair, Io the heifer who every morning restores daylight to men, to animals, to the mountains, the waters, the plants.

Signor Dido, on that extremely warm evening in the middle of July, heard the family clock strike ten; he thought that his duty as a good son had been prolonged beyond the necessary limit.

He knocked on his mother's door.

The grand baroness was about to go to bed.

The young baroness, Signor Dido's wife, was in the Piedmont for a week, visiting one of her sisters, along with their little daughter.

The old signora made a dash across the room, like a young girl surprised at her bath. She was wearing a Scheherazade dressing gown, and from inside the foaming lace emerged the hands of a tortoise and the neck of a fighting cock. On her head was a handkerchief knotted at the four corners—a sign that she had taken off her wig. In response to her son's good night, she averted her face and spluttered—a sign that she had taken out her dentures.

Signor Dido lived near the Porte de Versailles. He made his way to Montparnasse on foot. Even the *transports en commun* were celebrating that night of the 14th of July.

At every intersection, men and women, holding each other at a distance, serious, avoiding each other's eyes, performed a hopping dance, as if in a laborious reeducation of the lower limbs. The musicians, on a sort of revolutionary tribunal, repeated to infinity a dance tune from the time of President Fallières.

Between the Dôme and the Rotonde, Signor Dido had to elbow his way through men in shirtsleeves and suspenders and women blinded by their own hair, which smelled of sun-warmed hemp.

The place was brightly lit. The sum of streetlights, café lights, the Venetian lanterns drawn in festoons from one sidewalk to the other.

All at once Signor Dido felt an extraordinarily more intense source of light behind him.

He turned around.

He pretended not to see. He quickened his pace.

He had met Mary two or three times in the house of his brother the painter; they had exchanged a dozen words in all—and with studied detachment.

Mary called his name.

Alone? . . . She, too, was alone. Bronislaw was in London.

A sort of swimming began. Effortless. Unobstructed. A swimming in dreams.

So this meeting was the conclusion of a long story? How long had they known each other? . . .

Alone—in the midst of the crowd, the dancing, the voices, the music, the noise. Alone . . .

Enclosed in some ineffable insulation, in some miraculous gelatin.

People—life—how vulgar, stupid, ridiculous!

Mary spoke like a clear stream. And his soul glided into that stream.

When had Signor Dido ever given his heart with such confidence—and wrapped in such rectitude?

What had become of that embarrassment that put Signor Dido into a frozen state every time he found himself face-to-face with a woman?

Of that embarrassment there was barely a trace. Signor Dido had gone out with very little money in his pocket.

Had the divine Mary guessed it?

They strolled from café to café. Like sleepwalkers. Displeased with the ambience. In search of an ambience "worthy of them."

Which? . . . In each new café, to the expectant waiter, under the anxious silence of Signor Dido, the luminous voice repeated: "Un café crème." Signor Dido drew a breath of relief.

If they moved closer together? He sensed a warmth, an odor . . . So even this creature of light palpitated, perspired.

They came out as if from a dream: the dancing had stopped, the music was spent.

They walked.

Mary lived in a *pavillon*. A separate house. There are no doormen in *pavillons*.

They talked and talked in front of the open door.

He glimpsed an umbrella hanging from a coatrack, the foot of a staircase.

A thought flashed in Signor Dido. To cross that threshold, to kick the door shut behind him.

A dreadful thought.

Had anything shown on his face?

Dawn was coming.

When Signor Dido turned the corner with a last wave of the hand, all weight left him. He flew.

The night wind, too, has died down; the curtains hang still.

No passers-by. No rapid breath of automobiles.

1931. Signor Dido makes a quick calculation: twenty years . . .

Who had brought Signor Dido that news? And did the brain tumor refer to Mary or Bronislaw?

Berenice's hair is spread out behind Signor Dido's eyelids.

The luminous hair is parted at the top of a minuscule, black head. Big only in its hollow eyes, its exposed teeth.

And strand by strand the hair goes out.

A Strange Family

SIGNOR DIDO IS A PAINTER. TO ONE of his paintings he has given the name *A Strange Family*. It shows a family: father, mother, daughter. The pose of a group before the photographer's lens. The father in a frock coat and standing (approximate era: 1905). The mother in the middle, the daughter to the right: both seated. The daughter on the verge of spinsterhood, which she combats by means of gauzy blouses and big ribbons at her waist and in her hair. The mother going on fifty (the fifty of 1905, far different from the fifty of today: *cette jeunesse*), that is, the age at which a woman, by rubbing her face with cucumber, assiduously correcting her eyelashes, cheeks, and lips, and smoothing out her network of wrinkles, transformed herself into a taffeta woman: shiny and rustling. The father a commendatore.

This is the group that forms the *Strange Family*. But, put like that, the group of the Strange Family has nothing strange about it.

The strangeness is in their faces. It *comes from* their faces. From that sort of banana that bars the father's face; from the eye that swells like the entrance to an anthill on the mother's face; from the eyes that protrude like celestial ping-pong balls from the eye sockets of the daughter.

Those who have seen this picture and arrived at a judgment of it are divided into two categories: those, and they are the majority, who say that these strangely eczematous faces have no other reason for being than that of making Signor Dido pass for an original painter; and those few who, knowing Signor Dido well, have taught themselves to understand the legitimacy and profundity of these strange representations.

Which are said to be strange, but in fact are the exact representation of the truth.

I will explain myself.

Man looks at the men and things around him and believes he sees them, but in truth he does not see them. Instead he sees so many fixed schemes of men and things that he carries inside him, which together form his personal and idealistic representation of the world.

What is wrong with this believing one sees while not seeing? Think of a policeman who, even in the most inveterate criminals, goes on seeing honest men and nothing but honest men.

Like a policeman of humanity and the world, Signor Dido is not an idealist. Whether by training or by innate faculty, he sees men and things beyond the veil of idealism. Not always (that would be frightening): sometimes. Then men and things reveal their—how shall I say?—archaeological aspect. Better: their profound aspect. Signor Dido, in other words, reveals what might be called the *psychism of forms*.

Men and things, seen in this way, are not beautiful. But for Signor Dido this lack of beauty does not matter. On the contrary. It makes him love men and things even more deeply. A sort of leper's kiss.

Yesterday Signor Dido went to visit Colle del Cardinale, in the neighborhood of Perugia. At lunch, in the home of relatives, he met a gentleman and lady who said to him: "On your way back come and find our little house in Quercia. We'll have a bite together. The brat will be there, too."

Signor Dido did not catch the names of this gentleman and lady. He noted that the gentleman was called "Dottore."[1] How many *dottores* are there in Italy?

Signs whose nature it is still impossible to determine alert Signor Dido whenever he is about to come in contact with the psychism of forms.

So it was with the looks of this gentleman and lady.

Signor Dido and Signora Dido set out in their Topo,[2] visited Colle del Cardinale, and coming back in the mild twilight, among lushly wooded hills, set about searching for this Quercia.

The Topo, if one may put it so, groped its way.

Night fell.

Signor Dido stopped, inquired about the "Dottore's" house. Of a group of men sitting on a low wall in the dark, one stood up and, raising his fist in Signor Dido's direction, shouted: "Long live the proletariat!" From which Signor Dido deduced that his Topo, small and black, parked at the side of the road, was unequivocal evidence of plutocratism.

Once the smoke of this political gunshot scattered, Signor Dido, maneuvering with skillful gentleness, succeeded in finding out that, to reach the "Dottore's" house, one had to go uphill to the left fifty meters on, and then, after another two hundred meters, turn right, arriving at a gate between two high columns.

The Topo's tires grated on the gravel of the dark ascent.

Signor Dido went the presumed fifty meters, but found no crossroad either left or right. He went further: nothing.

Signor Dido stopped the Topo, began a difficult movement in reverse with his hand on the brake and the risk of rolling into the invisible abyss, and after Signora Dido had gotten out—not from fear, but, as she said, "to make the car lighter."

Signor Dido went down a little way on foot and stopped.

His eyes became accustomed to the dark. A white form moved a few steps away. Came closer: the white shirt of the "Dottore."

The Dottore was calm and at the same time astonished. Not find his house? Nothing could be easier!

He got behind the wheel himself. Stepped on the gas. The Topo took off at such speed as it had never dared or managed to reach under Signor Dido's guidance.

The Dottore swerved, plunged the Topo around the side of the hill.

The hill swallowed up the Topo, sucked it in through a black trench.

"Won't you turn on the headlights?" Signor Dido risked asking.

"No need," replied the Dottore. "It's such an easy road . . ."

The race up the dark slope continued at an insane speed and with dizzying curves. Signora Dido, in the back seat, was not breathing. Perhaps she had fainted.

"Here we are," said the Dottore. And the Topo came boiling to a stop.

"Here where?" thought Signor Dido.

They walked through the dark until Signor Dido stumbled.

"The stairs," said the Dottore.

When his eyes became accustomed to the light, Signor Dido found himself in the midst of a strange family. Not the one he had depicted: one of the many strange families scattered over the world.

"We never have anyone come here," the Dottore explained. "But you are something else. I've read your books. Followed your writings. You'll understand the reason for this refuge of ours. Most convenient at that. Only a few kilometers from the city. And you've seen what an easy road it is. We come here every evening. In certain periods we spend whole weeks here. Now that school's over, the brat doesn't go down to the city anymore."

The brat was a little boy of about nine, sitting on a seat shaped like a swan. He had fixed eyes and a sort of horn on his head.

"What's your name?" asked Signora Dido.

"I won't tell you," replied the brat. "I don't like my name."

"What nonsense!" said the mother, sitting on a seat shaped like a drum. "His name is Clodio."

"Why, that's a beautiful name!" said Signora Dido. And at the brat's grimace she added: "Would you like to be called Andrea?"

Andrea is Signor Dido's name, hence for Signora Dido it is the most beautiful name in the world.

"No," the brat replied firmly. "Andrea's a woman's name."

"What relaxation here!" the Dottore picked up again. "The rest that people allow themselves is never complete. It's not enough to take off your shoes and tie. You have to take off everything you put on yourself in order to resemble other people: to camouflage yourself. Complete rest is self-recovery."

A brief pause.

"Me, for example. In the city, I run an electrical engineering shop. But I'm not an electrical engineer: I'm a musician. That's my true nature. Up here I recover myself. You're also a musician, aren't you?"

"Somewhat," whispered Signor Dido.

"I know," said the Dottore. "One of your ballets was recently staged with success at La Scala. For another, no, but for you . . ."

The Dottore took from a cupboard an object shaped like a xylophone, placed it on the table that stood in the middle of the room, and on which Signor Dido would have preferred to see a tablecloth descend and plates be set out, some empty, others laden with foodstuffs.

The Dottore began to squeeze between his fingers, now one by one, now two together, the wooden cylinders that lay across the hollow of this strange instrument, and to shake them.

His face lit up; he rolled his eyes, undulated his body, moaned like an orchestra conductor in action.

His wife and the brat gazed at him in rapture.

The Dottore came to the end of this music without sound and fell wearily onto a chair.

"Beautiful!" said Signor Dido. "What is it?"

"My latest composition," replied the Dottore. "I call it *Music of the Spheres*. Pythagoras explained it. We don't hear the sublime music that the worlds make in their harmonious movement. Why? Because we hear it all the time."

A thump on the ceiling was heard.

"Grandma," said the brat.

"We won't be eating tonight," said the lady sitting on the drum. "I put two pizzas in the oven. But Tullio played *Music of the Spheres*, and the pizzas went watery."

What she meant by saying that on account of her husband's soundless music the pizzas went watery, Signor Dido was unable to find out.

Meanwhile the "complete rest" was at work.

Once social restraints are relaxed, the depth of the psyche expands freely, and frees forms at the same time. Noses lengthen into proboscises; eyes flow into globes of gelatin; lips round themselves into gimlets.

When Signor Dido and Signora Dido found themselves in their hotel, Signor Dido, who was subject to cardiac dysfunctions, felt a certain agitation in his chest and thought it prudent to take a sedative.

He looked for the little tube of Tefapal, but did not find it.

"What are you looking for?" Signora Dido asked him from the bed.

Signor Dido did not reply at once, because to say that one has need of medications is to confess a minor disgrace.

But on the other hand, what to do? Signor Dido plucked up his courage:

"I'm looking for the Tefapal."

"Let me do it," said Signora Dido, and she started going around the room in her nightgown.

Signora Dido moved with such circumspection that even this time Signor Dido did not manage to discover where Signora Dido had hidden the Tefapal from him.

A wife, says Signora Dido, is her husband's collaborator. To justify this affirmation, Signora Dido hides from her husband the objects that are necessary for him, so that, in order to have them, Signor Dido has to turn to her each time.

To requests for payment, and to them alone, does Signora Dido not say: "Let me do it."

The House on the Hill

SIGNOR DODI, IN HIS LITTLE CONVERTIBLE with the top down, is driving very slowly up the hill.

A stupendous morning.

At the foot of the hill flows the wide, peaceful river. Beyond the river stretches the city; on this side of the river rounds the hill, lush with vineyards, dotted with houses.

Having reached the top, Signor Dodi stops.

A house stands on the top of the hill. A two-storied house, surrounded by well-combed flowerbeds.

All the windows are open.

"From there," thinks Signor Dodi, looking at the second-story windows, "from there who knows what a marvelous view you enjoy."

At a second-story window, a white muslin curtain flutters a little and then hangs motionless.

Signor Dodi is a bachelor. He is about to turn sixty. For forty years now he has been feeding himself on projects. He thinks of a form of happiness, studies it, savors it: at the point of putting it into practice, he stops and postpones it.

Signor Dodi looks at the house on top of the hill, its open windows. He thinks:

"Here is the house of conjugal happiness. What time is it? Ten. *He* has gone down to the city. He doesn't need to work, but every man *has to do something*. Otherwise what kind of man is he?"

He, Signor Dodi, does not do anything, has never done anything. But he, Signor Dodi, it is not known why, he himself does not know why, places himself outside the common category. A sort of authorized outlaw.

"*She*," Signor Dodi goes on thinking, "*she* is still in the bathroom. Mature, soft, slightly fat."

The thought of this unknown and mature beauty shut up in the bathroom to do her *toilette* excites Signor Dodi a little. Oh, no! If Signor Dodi has not taken a wife, it is not for the same reasons that others do not take wives—Oscar Wilde, for instance.

"The babies," Signor Dodi goes on thinking, looking at the house on top of the hill. "Why babies? Children. The children are in school. They will return to the house in papa's car. In the kitchen, the cook is tightly trussing up the veal roast and pricking it with lard. In the bedrooms, the chambermaid is making the beds. This house seems empty; but the truth is that inside it is filled with quiet domestic labor.

"At one o'clock he comes back from the city, finds his wife . . . I find my wife, we sit down at the table . . ."

At the same moment as Signor Dodi is about to complete his imaginary conjugal happiness, a howl comes from the window with the white curtain.

Signor Dodi, frozen on the seat of his little convertible, thinks: "A werewolf."

Signor Dodi thinks, more precisely: "A lycanthrope." This "blank" man, this enemy of all care, of all responsibility, likes fine talk.

Has he heard right?

The howl is repeated: longer.

It is repeated again: more frequently.

What sort of maw does this howl come from?

To go into the house, to bring help, does not even occur to Signor Dodi.

Signor Dodi looks at the road ahead of him: nobody. He looks in the mirror at the road behind him: nobody.

Signor Dodi ducks down anyway to hide himself, releases the brake, shifts into gear, steps on the accelerator.

Steps harder than necessary. The roar of the engine drowns out the howling.

The exhaust pipe behind the little car going down the hill sends out a cloud of black smoke.

The howls are repeated ever more frequently.

Not from any maw: they come from the mouth of the engineer Ozieri.

The engineer Ozieri is in an armchair: at the far end of the room, in front of the open window, in front of the muslin curtain that flutters a little and then hangs motionless.

Unlike the muslin curtain, the engineer Ozieri is not moving. For five years now, Parkinson's disease has robbed him of all voluntary movement.

The engineer Carlo Ozieri was strong, vigorous, a ladies' man. The houses he built, white, tall as towers amidst the old, gray houses of the city, can even be seen from here. And now he is of one body with the armchair.

At the engineer's first howl, someone usually comes into the room, approaches him, takes him by both hands, and raises his arms in large circular gestures, like an Arab invoking Allah.

This time no one comes into the room.

Why?

Sometimes, at his howl, the engineer's wife herself—Signora Stella—comes into the room. But rarely.

Signora Stella is gigantic. Her face is broad and lifeless. A sort of corn silk sprouts on top of her head and hangs down in a fringe over her forehead.

Signora Stella is a busy woman. Since the engineer and the armchair became of one body, it is she who has "kept things going."

Now, too, Signora Stella is traveling around for her import-export business.

Signora Stella is drowning in work. She sleeps very little. When she is not sleeping or working, she practices spiritism: she calls up her son, executed in Forty-three at the age of seventeen.

At the engineer's howl, it is usually Signora Clelia who comes into the room, takes the engineer's hands, and raises his arms in big circular gestures, like an Arab invoking Allah.

Now, at the engineer's repeated howls, no one, not even Signora Clelia, comes into the room.

Why?

In the engineer's expressionless face, the pupils move anxiously from right to left. What are they searching for?

Even before Signor Dodi drove up the hill in his little convertible, even before he stopped to contemplate the house and from that contemplation drew dreams of conjugal happiness, inside the house, in the bathroom, there was indeed a woman doing her *toilette*; but it was not *his wife*, as Signor Dodi thought: it was Signora Clelia.

Signora Clelia heard a knock.

"Who is it?"

From outside the voice of Paolo shouted:

"Quick, Mama! It's Papa!"

Paolo is Signora Clelia's son. He is fourteen years old, has straight hair, sturdy bare legs, dirty knees.

Paolo is a little volcano. An "inventive" volcano. He regularly fails his examinations. Not in the subjects of study: in conduct.

Signora Clelia also has a daughter of twenty-three: Celestina. Two years ago Celestina married an engineer, and they left together for South Africa.

Signora Clelia married at the age of twenty. A man younger than herself: a boy. Children were born.

Ten peaceful years.

One day Signora Clelia felt a disturbance. Signora Clelia had read Dostoevsky. She thought: "We must be above that." Like a mother with her son, she invited her husband to confide in her.

They did not succeed in being above that. An infernal life began. One day Signora Clelia took her son and left the house. Changed cities. Took refuge with her friend Stella. They had been brought up together, like sisters. She helped Stella by dedicating herself to the sick man. Even as she raised the engineer's arms in large circular gestures, she never stopped thinking of him, over yonder. And she waited. Waited for the black dream to break up all at once.

When?

"Quick, Mama! It's Papa!"

The bathroom dances around Signora Clelia. The towels dance. Soapy nympheas dance over the water in the bathtub. The faucets dance. The flexible tube of the shower dances. The heart dances in Signora Clelia's breast.

In the midst of all this dancing, Signora Clelia thinks: "I must do my hair . . . Make myself up a little . . . If he sees me like this . . ."

But she cannot bear it: she slips into her bathrobe and goes flying down the stairs.

Paolo is rolling on the ground. Kicking his sturdy bare legs. Shaking with laughter. He shouts rhythmically: "April fool! April fool!"

Signora Clelia quickly glances around, collapses without a word.

Paolo no longer laughs. He stares wide-eyed at his mother on the ground, at the pinkish foam under her chin. Through the bathrobe, which has fallen open, he tries hard not to look. He repeats softly:

"Why? . . . It's April first . . . A joke . . . Why? . . ."

Howls come down from the room with the curtain.

That it was April first not even Signor Dodi was aware, absorbed as he was in his projects for conjugal happiness.

At the bottom of the slope, the smoke from the exhaust pipe gradually disperses.

The Feeling of Ravenna

SIGNOR DIDO RACES OVER THE BEAUTIFUL roads of Italy aboard
a little car of minimum cylinder capacity. To his right sits Signora
Dido.

Race, with regard to Signor Dido's automobilistic deambula-
tions, is an inappropriate word. Automobilism, in Signor Dido's
vocabulary, does not mean the mania for speed: it means passing
in review the spectacles of nature and of human labor while sitting in an armchair which has four wheels under it and moves by
its own propulsion.

On overtaking Signor Dido's little car, other motorists cast a
glance at him which has the air of saying: "Why don't you stay
home, old boy, instead of cluttering up the roads with that jalopy?"

These people don't know.

They don't know that Signor Dido loves the present more than
the past. They don't know that things in formation attract Signor
Dido's attention more lovingly than things already formed and
petrified. They don't know that living music, even dodecaphonic,
a living painter, even abstractionist, arouse Signor Dido's interest
far more than all the madrigalists and ignotes of the fourteenth
century put together.

And they—they race at high speed towards death and are already dead, and yet they look at him, Signor Dido, as a dead man!

Yesterday morning Signor Dido was racing along the road that goes from Rimini to Ferrara. He saw to his right a sign that read: Ravenna. He said to Signora Dido: "Let's stop in Ravenna." He said it without fervor.

Signor Dido feels himself borne along by the present as by a river. He loves those who share the same river with him, his river companions: he loves them out of solidarity, even those he hates. But does Signor Dido hate anyone? . . . Signor Dido has no time to hate. To hate means to have time to waste.

Signor Dido entered Ravenna. Entered by the Porta Garibaldi. And Ravenna had a strange effect on him.

All cities, even the most bashful, have a point, a marketplace or popular quarter, in which the city's insides emerge. But not Ravenna. Ravenna is buttoned up to the Adam's apple in its suit of stone. Or so Signor Dido saw it.

Signor Dido passed right through Ravenna without realizing it. On one street corner he found written: Via Anastagi.

This encounter pleased Signor Dido. It pleased him because it reminded him of Nastagio degli Onesti, the tragic ride through the pinewood of Chiassi, before the young men and women gathered for dinner.[1]

Nastagio, or Anastagio, or Anastasio: the Risen One.

To set out all together on the river of the Present: that is life for Signor Dido. And when the river of the Present flows into the tunnel called the Past, to enter all together into death: that is love for Signor Dido.

Signor Dido and Signora Dido went into a restaurant with a hotel above it. Sat at a small table. Foreigners of various races, various sexes, and various ages were sitting at the other tables. They were tugging at spaghetti, lasagna, fettuccine: they diligently introduced it into their mouths, as if setting about to learn Italian by means of food.

A young man in a windbreaker and dark glasses came into the restaurant and said in a loud voice: "Une heure quarante-cinq: visite aux monuments. A quarter to two: visit to the monuments. Altdenkmäln-Besuch um ein viertel vor zwei."

The foreigners sitting at the tables stood up as one man and filed out to visit the monuments.

Signor Dido thought: "I've finished eating: I ought to go and re-evoke the history of Ravenna through its monuments." And at this thought he felt unhappy.

It's not that Signor Dido has no love of history: he loves it but prefers to look at it through a keyhole.

Signor Dido looked, while Signora Dido was dexterously flaying a fish for him, looked at the history of Ravenna through a keyhole. He saw a dining room: not the one in which he found himself: another one. The dining room of the emperor Honorius.[2] Honorius, too, is sitting at the table, but he has no wife dexterously flaying a fish for him.

A nuncio comes into the room. He is out of breath. He raises his right hand in salute, as seen in films on Roman subjects. He says: "The barbarians have taken Roma!"

Honorius, though weak of character, leaps to his feet.

"Roma? But I fed her with my own hands half an hour ago!"

The nuncio doesn't understand at first. Then he understands and adds:

"I don't mean Roma, Your Majesty's favorite hen. I mean the Urbe."

"Dimwit!" exclaims the augustus, his face quite reassured, dropping into his chair again and going back to his meal of parrots' tongues. "You might have told me so at once!"

Signor Dido went from the restaurant to the hotel, had them give him a cool room, took a magnificent nap.

And dreamed. Dreamed of his friend Enrico. And whom else would Signor Dido have dreamed of in Ravenna?

Enrico first saw the light in Ravenna a little less than fifty years ago. His father was a restorer of mosaics. And to Enrico, as the most gifted of his three sons, he thought to hand on the secrets of this difficult and painstaking art.

Father and son would leave by the Porta Garibaldi while it was still night, cross the Canale del Molino Lovatelli, and set out over the fields in the direction of Sant'Apollinare in Classe, where at that time important restoration work was being carried out.

Halfway there they would stop at a tavern. It was an enormous black room, in the middle of which danced the flames of a brazier.

Father and son would sit at a table. The clients brought raw food and cooked it in the common skillet set on the brazier.

Among those morning clients there was also the dogcatcher, who would take a piece of meat from his haversack and toss it into the frying pan; and even the most inexperienced of zoologists would recognize in that piece of meat the haunch of a dog. There was also the snake catcher, but he ate cold. He would take a snake from his shoulder bag, hold it up live and squirming between his fingers, dip the tip into the bowl of salt placed in the middle of the table, bite it off, and chew it.

Enrico passed through childhood, adolescence; he became one of the most gifted adults that Signor Dido has ever known. And variously active: painter, architect, writer, conceiver of infinite plans, but always frowned upon by fate.

Enrico, now, after working so much, after conceiving so much, after planning so much, is poor and sick. He lives in a corridor, under the roof of an old and illustrious Roman palazzo; a corridor which, by means of a play of blankets stretched between the walls, he has turned into a soft labyrinth, a soft and wavering labyrinth, which a little girl crosses and re-crosses like a little dancing light: Donnina, Enrico's daughter, a child of five for whom, if he had known her, Mozart would have written a little work of his most subtle and scintillating music.

Signor Dido came out of this dream while it was still broad daylight.

"And the monuments?" asked Signora Dido.

"Yes," replied Signor Dido. "Let's go to visit Dante's tomb."

What is poetry? Signor Dido does not know how to answer this question. But Dante, thinks Signor Dido, Dante is extraordinary above all for this, that he transforms speech into sculpted form. Others model with their hands. Dante models with his tongue and lips, and from his mouth, however pinched and puckered, shaped marble issues in a long ribbon.

Coming from the mouth of Dante, even useless things acquire value. Such as that mountain pointed out as the obstacle that prevented the inhabitants of Pisa and Lucca from looking at each other, when it would have been much more expedient simply to name it.

In order to approach Dante's tomb, Signor Dido had to get out of the car. Chains hung in festoons from post to post keep vehicles from approaching the tomb of the Most High Poet.

"Dante," thought Signor Dido, "Dante sleeps here. I, on the other hand, in my ground-floor flat in Rome, not only sleep but also work twelve hours a day. Yet no one even dreams of making the vehicles that go roaring past my windows and addle my brain keep a little farther away."

On the face of the tomb Signor Dido reads: DANTIS POETAE SEPULCRUM.

Signor Dido reads and is amazed.

Why *poetae*? And why this Latin?

Dante is the most Italian of poets. He also wrote books in Latin. If he had written only books in Latin, he would be as remembered today as Petrarch is remembered for being the author of the *Africa*.

"And the musaics?" asked Signora Dido.

It was Signor Dido's intention to visit the famous mosaics of Ravenna. But Signora Dido did not say *mosaics*, she said *musaics*. And certain words act like billiard cushions on Signor Dido.

"What, don't you like musive art?" Signora Dido added, when she realized that Signor Dido was leaving the city.

Signor Dido accelerated. He left Ravenna without having visited the basilicas, without having visited the mausoleum of Galla Placidia, without so much as a glance at the Guidarello, though the Guidarello is not a musaic, but the masculine *pendant* of Ilaria del Carretto of Lucca.

"C'est égal," said Signora Dido, with a touch of bitterness in her voice. "C'est égal: to come to Ravenna and not see Sant'Apollinaire!"

Signora Dido loves the French poets of the last fifty years. The names of French poets of the last fifty years keep running pleasantly through her head.

Five Trees

SIGNOR DIDO IS IN BED.

What woke him up?

Signor Dido reaches his right hand out of bed, feels around for the clock, brings the luminous little quadrant close to his nose: four.

Outside it is still night.

What woke him up?

Signor Dido does not turn on the light. He "feels" that he should not turn it on. The reason that has awakened him so suddenly, but without nudging him, without startling him—does not want to be looked at in the light.

Signor Dido's bed is beside the window. The windowsill is level with the bed. It is as if Signor Dido is lying on the windowsill. He sees the garden down below him, the hedge at the back, the trees that raise up their slender columns; far away, beyond the foliage, the peaks of the Apuan Alps.

Signor Dido's country house is low and long. It is a horizontal house. Even the windows are horizontal.

What woke Signor Dido up in the middle of the night?

Signor Dido doesn't know, but he feels the cause there a few steps away. Alive.

Signora Dido sleeps at the other end of the house, in the room which, on the architect's plan, was the conjugal bedroom. But

Signor Dido is an artist: he writes, paints, composes music. And artists—so thinks Signora Dido—have need of isolation. She therefore placed Signor Dido's bed at the far end of the living room.

What woke Signor Dido up in the middle of the night?

Signor Dido turns his head to the left.

The window is a meter and a half from the ground. It is divided into nine rectangles of glass framed in wood. Only the middle rectangle opens.

Signor Dido attaches a moral rather than a practical purpose to work. Before lying down, he opens the middle rectangle and pushes the blinds aside. The daylight wakes him up, and he goes back early to the work interrupted the evening before.

By a high flash of lightning, far away, over the peaks of the Apuans, Signor Dido glimpses the trunks of the trees, each in its proper place.

There are two hundred and fifty-eight trees in the garden.

Signora Dido made this count in the summer of Forty-three. Then, in the summer of Forty-five, when, after a forced absence of two years, Signora Dido returned with some luck to her country house, she thought: "My poor trees! Imagine the slaughter!" She knew that for more than a year the war had settled here and there in the Cinquale. She knew that many pines had been chopped down to clear the way for artillery fire. She knew that, with the war over, the inhabitants of the place had cut down more trees to evaporate sea water and extract the salt from it.

With bated breath, Signora Dido went through the opening where the gate had been. The house was gutted, yes. But the trees? . . . Signora Dido counted them: two hundred and sixty-three. Five extra!

Lightning still flashes over the Apuans, or is it the first glimmer of dawn?

Signor Dido gradually begins to make out the trunks of the trees.

Then he gradually sees that the trunks of the trees are moving.

Does it mean there is a storm outside the window? A silent storm?

One of the trees approaches the window.

"Where have I seen that face before?" Signor Dido asks himself.

He recognizes it. It is that German soldier who came into his house on the thirteenth of September Forty-three, in canvas shorts, bare from the waist up, and waved a hundred-lira bill, and said with the voice of a talking dog: "I do not ropp: I puy your radio."

The German soldier is so close to the window that his white face touches the glass. His lips are moving, but Signor Dido does not hear anything.

The German's hand, as white as his face, makes a sign for him to open. Signor Dido opens the middle rectangle.

"Gut mornink," says the German.

"Good morning," Signor Dido replies from bed. "What brings you to these parts?"

"These parts? I never left these parts."

"Oh, come on!" Signor Dido rather sighs than says out loud.

"Never left," repeats the German, "and now your picture is returned to you."

"My picture?"

"*The Roman Empire.*"

At that name, a light went on in Signor Dido's mind.

In September of Forty-three, when Signor Dido had had to abandon his country house in all haste, because the Germans were camped in his garden and, under the pretext of taking water from the pump and washing their clothes, wandered through the house day and night, he had left the house as it was: furniture, linens, crockery; and six pictures on the walls besides, painted by himself.

Each of the six pictures had its title: *Hector and Andromache*, *Crete*, *Orpheus*, *Vera*, *Holy Friday*, *The Roman Empire*.

Except for *Vera*, which was the portrait of Vera Cacciatore Signorelli,[1] they were all pictures with stories.

Nowadays they say, "Painting is not literature." But Signor Dido lets them talk, and goes on calmly and faithfully painting pictures suggested to him by his fantasy.

Orpheus portrayed a man who had a lyre in place of a head. In *Holy Friday* an enormous black hammer crashed down on the floor of a church filled with vesperal shadow. The picture entitled *Crete* showed the Minotaur clutching the labyrinth to his breast. In *Hector and Andromache* the Trojan hero said good-bye to his wife, and though he knew he would lose his hide in the duel with Achilles, revealed in his smile a wall of equine teeth between two protruding lips, formed by four castor oil capsules, two above and two below, reddened with carmine.

Then, in the summer of Forty-five, when Signor Dido went back to his country house, he found amidst the rubble the punctured, scorched remains of five of his pictures, but of *The Roman Empire*, which was the biggest of all, and hung alone on the far wall of the living room, he found no trace.

The surviving pictures, restored as well as possible, Signor Dido had hung back on the walls, like so many relics. The sixth relic was missing.

"Are you looking for your picture *The Roman Empire?*" asked the German.

Signor Dido nodded.

The German told the following story:

The German soldiers hardly looked at the other pictures that hung on the walls. But the picture that bore the title of *The Roman Empire*, plainly visible on a little card attached to the frame, struck the German soldiers so much that they took it down from the wall and carried it to their house in the garden.

Has Signor Dido seen that big hole in the middle of the garden? That was the underground shelter that the German soldiers had dug for themselves in the depths of the earth, to hide at night from the shells that the American negroes rained down on them from the other side of the Cinquale. Until one night a shell fell directly on the house and . . .

The Roman Empire was the most beautiful ornament of the house. In the evening, before going to sleep, by the metallic light of acetylene, the German soldiers, wrapped up in their blankets, nearly split their sides laughing at that mounted Roman emperor with a calf's head, and those togaed senators, some with the heads of buzzards, some with the heads of bulldogs, some with the heads of hyenas.

"That comical image of your old Roman empire strengthened our faith in the great Germanic empire, which our Hitler was extending across Europe."

Signor Dido protested:

"I didn't make those animal-headed figures with any satirical intention. Quite the contrary: it's a psychological accentuation."

The German fixed on Signor Dido a blond gaze, which, though meant to be shrewd, was even more porcine than usual.

"Oh, sie, Spassmacher!"[2]

Signor Dido was about to press home his own arguments; but he thought: "The art critics themselves don't understand the meaning of these hybrid figures of mine; how should they be understood by this German soldier, night-bound, white as the bark of a poplar?"

"Basta!" snapped the German. "All finished now. Great German empire kaput. Oh, not because Germany lose the war: for cheocraphic reasons. Germany strong, when Germany was heart of Europe and Europe center of the world. Now that Europe no more center of the world . . ."

The soldier turned towards the back of the garden and fired a sort of command into the darkness: "Los, Jungens! Bringt das Bild von Herrn Dido her!"[3]

Four white tree trunks emerged from the darkness carrying *The Roman Empire*, two on one side and two on the other.

Signor Dido opened the French window. The four Germans, preceded by the one who had spoken, and who had the rank of corporal, brought the picture into the living room and hung it from the hook that was still there in the middle of the wall.

Unlike the other "casualties of war," *The Roman Empire* was intact.

The five Germans clicked their heels, saluted militarily, and went back into the night.

Anyone else would have been robbed of sleep by an adventure of that sort. Signor Dido fell back to sleep at once.

In the morning Signor Dido is awakened by the daylight. On the far wall there is no trace of the picture entitled *The Roman Empire*.

Signor Dido has a little bitch to whom, in spite of her sex, he has given the name of Puck. These days Puck is in such a condition that all the dogs of the neighborhood have surrounded Signor Dido's house.

Signor Dido puts the leash on Puck, and they go out together to take a turn around the garden.

They stop in front of the hole.

Puck scratches the dirt with her paws, growls, pulls at the leash.

What are these five trees that rise up tall around the hole? They look like poplars, but are not poplars: their trunks are whiter, slenderer; and the leaves up above, rather than green on one side and silvery on the other, are strangely flesh colored.

Are these the five extra trees Signora Dido found?

Signor Dido takes out a pocketknife, presses the blade against the bark.

Puck gives a tug at the leash and runs off squealing.

The leaves of the tree shudder slightly. As if from pain.

A Villa in Rapallo

HERE WE ARE IN RAPALLO FOR THE THIRD time in the space of a few weeks.

The second time was in early August and in full Amphitryonic fervor. This third time summer is going through *une seconde jeunesse*,[1] its fervor slightly cooled and already gilded by autumn.

The first time was around the twentieth of June. Rapallo was ready for action and very well supplied: it was awaiting the army of bathers.

Maître d's in tails and waiters in white jackets stood at attention behind ranks of spotless and deserted tables. The *parterres* were tilled. The flowerbeds were raked. The meadows were glittering with the best gifts of Flora. The shops were sparkling. The *concierges* on the doorsteps of the *hôtels* were prepared to start bowing. The furniture was polished, the curtains were variegated, maids in white crests stood watch, already set in that smile which is an irresistible refutation of the law of the fixed price.

Directors and managers, eyes to their telescopes, scanned the horizon.

Where was the army of bathers?

The fascination of waiting also took hold of me. I also waited. For three days I waited. But at the end of the third day I said to myself: "Who is making you do this?"

Then I remembered that my friend Pilade, the last time I saw him in Milan, had said to me: "If you pass through Rapallo, go to my villa. Your room is waiting for you. I've alerted Ido."

"Who is Ido?"

"The caretaker."

I sent the little car up a steep road, and after a dozen curves stopped at a gate.

Had I missed the way?

At the top of two columns, two terracotta dogs perpetuated the image of vigilance and loyalty.

Ido was about to take my suitcase.

I stopped him: "No. I'll just have a quick look at the engineer's collection of paintings and leave at once. Go on with your gardening. I'll manage by myself."

I went into the villa.

At that same instant, sixty years of life fell from my shoulders. I found myself a baby again. Smaller than a baby: a newborn. But I saw and reasoned as I see and reason now.

I easily became accustomed to the darkness preserved by the closed blinds, the locked shutters, the drawn curtains. To me, a child, that darkness was familiar. It was the darkness that lends poetry to a house, that protects it from the enemy sun. From the front hall a big stairway with a red runner opened out like an immense fan, flanked by curving banisters.

On reaching the upper floor, I opened a door.

A bedroom, obviously. Thick bed-curtains spilled down from a canopy; in a corner shone one of those big oval mirrors to which the French have given the name of Amor's lover: *Psyché*.

I was about to close the door again: a voice stopped me.

"Don't go away."

Beyond the bed I made out an armchair with enormous spiral ears. In the armchair something stirred.

The voice added:

"Sit down, please. We'll have a chat."

On the right side of the form that had spoken, a sort of arm moved to point me to the offered seat. This seat was half of an immense shell, held up by four arched dolphins, heads on the floor and tails on high.

"Are you a friend of the engineer's?"

"We've never met. When the engineer comes to Rapallo, I hide in the cellar. The engineer loves the modern. He bought this villa a couple of years ago, because he could have it at a modest price. I'm afraid that one day or other he'll throw out the furniture, scrape off the decorations, change everything. Then I'll have to find other lodgings."

Seeing him sunk so deeply in the armchair, I had taken him for a paralytic.

"So you can move?"

"Move? Why, I am movement personified."

He added more gently: "Ideal movement."

The strange personage rose from the chair: to put it better, he loosed upwards the curves, twists, ellipses, spirals, falling petals which together made up his vaguely anthropomorphic shape.

He went on:

"Men love movement. To put it better, they feel the universal movement and, in various ways, strive to honor it.

"Not always. Sometimes, distracted from natural life by various thoughts, man does not feel movement. So it was at the moment of the mosaics of Ravenna. The Renaissance could as well be called the Resuming of Contact with Movement.

"One must distinguish, however, between the intellectual representation of movement and direct participation in movement: the first is a form worthy of the intellectual animal known as man; the second is the activity of the stupid.

"The contemplation of movement in its various representations in the Victory of Samothrace, in the twining pictures of Rubens, in the corkscrew meters of Shakespeare, in the egg-whisk sculptures of Bernini, in the flourishes and cadenzas of musicians, while remaining at rest oneself, is for elegant and wise men.

"Thus one arrives at the Baroque, a most elegant and wise period, in which everything around man—buildings, furniture, art, decoration—is the representation of movement; one arrives at the florid, which, with its volutes, its spirals, its ellipses, was also a grand representation of movement around man at rest because the florid style, as you know, coincides with the acme of capitalist economy, which, for those who benefitted from that economy, was a perfect condition of elegance and wisdom."

I was about to contradict the theories of this strange personage; his verbal outpouring prevented me.

"Here we are on the Riviera," he continued. "In one of the paradises of the *rentiers*.[2] Look around: it's all still florid."

He was silent for a moment, then went on more gravely:

"And now? . . . Men, now, are neither elegant nor wise. They do not content themselves with contemplating representations of movement: they participate in movement themselves, and keep running faster and faster.

"The result? The more a man runs, the more his brain stands still. Never has the world around the running man been so flat, so still, so stupid as now."

After all, I thought, this unlikely personage reasons rather well.

But who is he?

"I am Mister Liberty.[3] The elder of the Liberty brothers."

"And from England you've turned up here on the Ligurian Riviera?"

"I find myself at home here. It's the last refuge of liberty."

"And your brother?"

"He's here, too. Didn't you see him? He'll be on the floor below."

I said good-bye to the elder of the Liberties and went downstairs.

As I passed through the living room, I glimpsed, lying on a *bergère* that formed an enormous petal, a spiral-shaped personage in every way similar to the personage with whom I had spoken on the floor above.

He was asleep.

Contemplating the representations of movement does not suit me after all. I prefer to move myself. I don't want to be either elegant or wise.

And I went out on tiptoe.

The Health Spa

THIS PAST JULY, SIGNOR AND SIGNORA Dido spent ten days at a famous health spa in the Dolomites.

A step up in the social life of Signor and Signora Dido.

One day, on the main street of the famous health spa, Signor Dido ran into Count P. Signor Dido praised the amenity of the place, the majesty of the mountains.

"We arrived an hour ago by car," said Count P. "We're stopping here for lunch and then we go on to Austria. We come here in the winter. To ski."

Signor Dido did not bat an eye, but a few analogies flashed through his mind: the difference between coming in the summer to a health spa in the Dolomites and coming in the winter to ski; the difference between swimming from a sandy beach and swimming off the rocks; the difference between hearing the *Passion According to Saint Matthew* sung in Italian and hearing it sung in German.

Signora Dido balks at the widespread custom of sending picture postcards to friends from places one happens to be passing through. Nevertheless, having arrived in the famous health spa in the Dolomites, Signora Dido bought many picture postcards, wrote greetings on them, signed them, and sent them to even the most distant and forgotten of her friends.

A few days later, Signora Dido received a picture postcard in her turn. It was from one of her distant acquaintances, a woman of modest circumstances. "Big kisses" was written on it, and it came from a health spa in the Dolomites no less famous than the one in which Signora Dido found herself.

An exhibition of paintings opened in the famous health spa.

Signor Dido went to see it. A few figure paintings, a few landscapes, many abstract paintings.

Signor Dido thought: "What is this phenomenon? For the Italian man, life is form. The Italian man knows that at the sounding of the sacred trumpets he will find himself back in his own body, and dressed in that body he will present himself before the judgment seat of God. So Luca Signorelli shows it in his fresco in the Duomo of Orvieto,[1] so Virgil says to Dante after Ciacco has finished speaking:

He will take back again his flesh and form.[2]

"Do Italian painters, then, no longer believe in the resurrection of the flesh? Has a revolution gone on in the heads of Italian painters similar to that which, more than four centuries ago, went on in the head of Doctor Luther? And what signs, apart from these straight lines, these curved lines, these spirals, these variously colored discs, attest to the actual occurrence of this revolution?"

Signor Dido did not answer his own questions. He just said, "Drop it." So he hears men, women, and children say as they pass by under his ground-floor window in Rome.[3]

Signor Dido is an expert in intellectual matters. He can distinguish by smell an intellectual expression moved by profound motives from an intellectual expression moved by nonprofound motives.

Drop it.

As Signor Dido passed and repassed in front of these straight lines, these curves, these spirals, these variously colored discs, he happened to cross paths several times with a woman of lofty stature and even loftier bearing.

And this woman was not abstract.

Or not entirely. In her eyes, slightly slanting like the eyes of the Sphinx, there was that touch of the abstract that one finds in the look that looks beyond things.

How did it happen?

A group formed. Mutual acquaintances got to work. Signor Dido was introduced to the woman with slanting eyes.

We are creatures of flesh and blood, and at the same time shades. In the woman with slanting eyes, Signor Dido recovered a piece of his own past.

Between 1916 and 1917. Thirty-four years ago. The woman with slanting eyes may not have come into the world yet, but her father was in the world: a famous psychiatrist who at that time, as a colonel in the medical corps, headed a military hospital some ten kilometers from Ferrara.

A big, dilapidated building known as the Seminary, from its former function as a school for priests. Hemp fields smoked all around it.

Art historians say that so-called metaphysical painting was born in that building.[4]

They are mistaken.

Signor Dido has other memories of the Seminary.

He remembers that soldier sheltered in the basement, who did not walk but advanced by sudden leaps, who did not talk but uttered brief, rolling cries like the gobbling of a turkey. His punctured head had been fitted with a black skullcap.

He remembers that lieutenant locked up in a little room on the ground floor, who shouted through the door to be let out. No, he wouldn't go looking for drugs. He was cured now. What? Can't they see he's cured?

He remembers, in a room on the second floor, at the end of the corridor . . .

Sick? Malingering?

He was in bed for ten months. He wore a miller's cap on his head. Around the bed, on bedside tables of white enameled iron, he had collected a polyglot's library. He was learning languages on his own. He mouthed the syllables with silent lips, now looking in the dictionary, now repeating from memory, gazing into space.

Night fell. The light fell in the rooms and corridors. The moon fell through the hemp smoke beyond the window.

The Seminary slept. Outside, in the fields, the orderlies made love to the girls from the neighboring farms. In the bluish corridor, the clinical polyglot, a skeleton in ghostly pajamas, paced rapidly up and down with inaudible steps. Now and then the turkey's gobbling came from the basement.

"And you, Signor Dido, what do you think of abstract painting?"

• • •

Past? Present? . . . A man turned into a turkey? A woman with slanting eyes? . . . Creatures of flesh and blood? Shades? . . .

The Kiss

LIKE SO MANY OTHERS, SIGNOR DIDO went to see the Caravaggio exhibition in Milan this past summer. Paintings of Caravaggio that Signor Dido had never seen in museums or churches. Gathered together, the work made a profound impression on him. Before this representation of things "as they are," dark and at the same time flashing like a thunderstorm, the Renaissance representation of things "as they ought to be" seemed all the more false to him. He marveled above all that things "as they are" could rise to such power, to such poetry. Is poetry, then, not beyond things "as they are," superior to things "as they are"? No one manages to escape this "theological" opinion of poetry, starting with those who negate it. Realism? Yes, but carried to its extreme. A mother's lament for the death of her children, for the destruction of her house under the blows of Roberto Bracco,[1] rivals the howling of Hecuba.

The rage to get to the roots of reality now devours Signor Dido.

Hidden were the sources of the Nile; hidden was the human soul. More hidden than the sources of the Nile and the human soul is the reality of things; and all the more hidden in that everyone thinks it is self-evident, obvious, easily within reach.

Signor Dido has mobilized his friends. He draws them, models them, paints them. And in each of them he seeks the root of *their own* reality. So that the insides of reality should appear on the canvas, that reality which not only the veiled eye of euphemism, but nature herself conceals; all the more so from a man veiled in euphemism.

Three days ago Signor Dido began the portrait of Professore Elvio.

Can it be called a portrait?

"Began" also won't do. The dash with which he sets out to pierce the appearance of reality and get to its roots makes the word "attack" more suitable.

Signor Dido felt the absence in this "portrait" of a very important element in the metaphysical reality of Professore Elvio: death.

A skull was needed. A real skull, perfectly round. Signor Dido now found it repugnant to work in a Mannerist way.

Professore Elvio said: "I have an idea," and went to make a telephone call.

Doctor Cerimele arrived in a taxi, a young physician, recently graduated. He was carrying a leather briefcase. Flat.

"What's in the briefcase? He must not have understood." So thought Signor Dido, and he became angry. Signor Dido is more and more intolerant of the small or large obstacles that block his way; and his way is becoming more and more a sort of personal film, an unbroken ribbon of his own desires, thoughts, and dreams, and of the realization of his own desires, thoughts, and dreams.

The young physician opened the briefcase and took out a skull. He held it up in his hand, showed it around, and placed it on the desk.

A little volley of jokes burst out. The two physicians and Signor Dido himself barely refrained from playing Hamlet.

The skull was small and in excellent condition. The teeth were perfect.

"No trace of cavities," noted Professore Elvio.

"What age was it?" asked Signor Dido.

"Twenty, twenty-five at the most. Look at the clarity of the sagittal. In old people the parietals fuse and the sagittal disappears."

"How long has it been dead?"

"Some twenty years. Perfect preservation, smooth bone."

Signor Dido went back to painting. He felt the orbital cavities fixed on the back of his neck from the desktop.

A man's look or a woman's?

This doubt gradually penetrated his mind like a soft nail.

He decided to ask Professore Elvio.

"No way to know. There are no sexual differences between a man's skull and a woman's."

Ccrimcle had left. Professore Elvio also left. Alone with himself, Signor Dido thought of putting the image of Death beside Professore Elvio's head. He placed the skull on the tip of a portable easel. He stuck the pointed tip of the easel into the large occipital foramen. He tipped the skull to one side, as if in confidential colloquy. Under the skull he draped a pink drapery.

Man or woman?

The sky darkened. It began to rain. One could no longer see to paint. Signor Dido drew the curtain over the window of the studio.

He went to have supper. Then withdrew to the studio again.

A progressive lack of stimuli for our soul; our soul so in need of stimuli, of replies to its continuous, insistent, "silent" questions; so in need of happiness.

What comes to us from the world? The resumption or nonresumption of negotiations in Korea; Persian oil; revisions of the

Diktat; Trieste and Zone B; the English on the Suez Canal . . .

And our mind goes on waiting.

Signor Dido tries to make up for this marasmus with poetry and philosophy. Poetry and philosophy have so far yielded good results. Even as arid a philosophy as the *Nicomachean Ethics*.

"This evening," thinks Signor Dido, "the *Divine Comedy* may yield me some beneficial effects." He takes the *Divine Comedy* from the bookshelf, like taking a bottle of vitamins from the medicine chest.

He gets into bed. He opens to the first cantos of the *Paradiso*. What verses he comes upon!

> These organs of the universe, then, go
> From grade to grade, as now thou see'st is done,
> For from above they take, but work below.[2]

He searches further ahead:

> So would a hound stand still between two does.[3]

Signor Dido knows that *dame* means *damme*, female deer: however, the image of a *chien dans un jeu de quilles* stays with him.[4]

Signor Dido raises his arm and flips the light switch.

Usually, when the switch is flipped, the light goes out. This time it shines more brightly.

From the back of the studio, the draped figure comes forward. It stops at Signor Dido's bedside.

"So you had doubts? Look at me. I'm a woman."

Her hair hangs free. Her body quivers under the drapery freed of ties and buttons.

The timidity which since adolescence has worked on Signor Dido's mind like Westinghouse brakes on the wheels of railway cars, works all the more strongly now insofar as he is in bed and this magnificent girl is standing before him. What's more, his pajamas are not very fresh. And to shield his hairless scalp from the chill of night, Signor Dido has pulled a woolen cap down to his ears.

"Who are you? How did you manage to get in? I bolted the door myself."

"Clown!" the girl shoots back. "Who am I? How did I manage to get in? . . . But your friend, that Professore Elvio, was wrong. I was thirty. And for thirty years I haven't grown any older. So we're the same age, you and I, though we look so different."

The girl bends down to Signor Dido, as if to talk with him in secret.

Signor Dido shrinks back against the wall.

"Softly, for goodness sake! My wife is asleep in there."

The girl bursts into laughter, which bares her teeth. Extremely white, even; too white, in fact, and too even; the teeth of a horse, the teeth of a . . .

"And you even pretend you don't recognize me! Don't you remember the magnificent words you said to me, the magnificent phrases you wrote to me? I've kept all your letters here, under this sort of pink peplum you yourself put on me . . . See if you recognize me now!"

The girl throws herself full length on Signor Dido and presses her mouth to his mouth.

So sweet—so unbearable: the kiss you're *not prepared for.*

Either from this unprepared-for kiss, or from fear that the door would open and Signora Dido would appear in her nightgown, Signor Dido takes hold of the girl's head, tears it from him, pushes it away.

And the head falls.

It is still rolling about in two pieces when Signor Dido turns on the light.

Signor Dido picks up one piece and sets it on the desk. The other had ended up who knows where.

In the morning Vittoria came into the studio. Signor Dido asked her to sweep under the bookcase.

Vittoria drew the other half of the skull from under the bookcase. Along with it came the corpse of a cockroach and three olive pits.

Signor Dido is a glutton for olives.

From time to time Signora Dido buys him some olives, but, in order to dole them out to him herself, she hides them in a place known only to her.

Signor Dido has discovered the hiding place. At night he goes and steals olives. To remove the traces of his guilt, he throws the pits under the bookcase.

The Pizza

It is Christmas day.

Signor Dido is on the train that leaves Syracuse at 7 AM and arrives in Rome at 9:30 PM.

The train bears the title of an express.

This is the first time that Signor Dido has found himself on a train on Christmas day.

Signor Dido is savoring the advantages of this singular journey.

It is in the literal meaning of "singular" that the felicitous character of this journey lies.

The Syracuse–Rome express carries only one first-class car, and this car carries only one traveler: Signor Dido himself.

To enjoy the advantages of his solitary journey even more, Signor Dido thinks of life as it unfolds for people on this same day at home in the bosom of their families. He thinks of the full family, enriched by "added" relations. He thinks of festive clothes. He thinks of the tip for the doorman and the exchange of good wishes. He thinks of the longer than usual meal, the laborious digestion, the empty afternoon.

Whereas on the train . . .

A conductor had appeared in the compartment, had taken the ticket from Signor Dido's hand, had examined it, punched it, and handed it back without offering a word. The functionary's footsteps had gone down the corridor, had reentered the roar of the train. And Signor Dido thought: "A wave forms on the surface of the sea, runs on solitarily, reenters the sea."

To the right the mountains of Calabria unroll one after another and roll back up again; the sea to the left extends motionlessly under the sun.

Christmas.

Signor Dido again picks up the newspaper bought in Sicily, rereads for the fourth time some news items totally lacking in interest, turns to put it down on the empty seat.

Boredom here, too, but without constraints. Boredom free in itself. And nature all around—sky, earth, sea—nature transformed entirely into an immense divan, in the middle of which he, Signor Dido, jounces solitarily to the jouncing of the wheels.

The family dinner, the voices, the laughter, the confusion: like finding yourself in the rain without an umbrella. Yes. But when your stomach begins to growl in the silence under your cardigan . . .

Having crossed the Strait, the train had maneuvered onto the tracks of Villa San Giovanni, and Signor Dido, leaning out the window, had watched with childish avidity the coupling of the dining car to his own car.

"The dining car!"

"How many sittings?" Signor Dido asked in return.

The employee in the brown uniform did not answer aloud: he spread his arms in a gesture of submission. And Signor Dido, the enemy of ready-made phrases, recognized that even he was sometimes the victim of ready-made phrases.

Signor Dido went lurching down the corridor and through the accordion passage between the cars.

Only three tables were set. At one an elderly and thin married couple, at the other a middle-aged woman.

Signor Dido goes to sit at the third table. He turns the glass mouth-up, pinches the bread roll, looks circumspectly at the middle-aged woman.

"How come alone on Christmas day?"

He looks closer.

"This woman is rich in appetites but lacking in sentiments."

He adds:

"Of this type of woman, the French say: *Elle a les foies blancs.*"[1]

The waiter, with the gestures of a tightrope walker, takes away the plate on which Signor Dido has finished eating rice and peas.

From the door opposite the one through which Signor Dido entered, a man comes into the dining car.

A man of about thirty. Olive-skinned. Thick of hair and pelt. Blue-jowled. Big almond eyes. The placid gaze of a ruminant. Clothes stretched over bundles of muscles.

He sits at a table across the aisle, level with Signor Dido. He indicates the bare table with his hand.

The waiter spreads a tablecloth, sets down before the latecomer two superimposed plates, silverware, glasses.

"Wine!" orders the traveler.

The waiter comes back with a small bottle of wine, uncorks it, places it on the table.

The traveler grasps a package that he has placed under his seat, unwraps it, pulls out a pizza folded like a wallet, and spreads it on the plate.

An enormous pizza. It completely covers the plate, its edges touch the tablecloth. Its top is red with tomatoes, silvery with anchovies.

The traveler nails the pizza down with a perpendicular fork and begins cutting around it; he studies each slice with his placid eye, stuffs it into his mouth, swelling out his cheeks, and chews with a methodical rotation of the jaw.

The waiter, who comes from the far end of the car holding a plate of rice and peas, stops in perplexity.

Observed from behind by the waiter, the traveler with the pizza goes on chewing methodically.

The waiter, overcoming his perplexity, resumes his advance with a hunter's tread.

In Signor Dido's mind a story by Dostoevsky entitled *The Double* replays itself.

The waiter continues to advance.

Signor Dido read that story many years ago, but, like all things by Dostoevsky, it was stamped in his memory with an indelible imprint.

The waiter advances.

It is about a certain man who sees himself—the Double—in the most shameful situations: naked in the midst of a room full of people in evening dress, spat upon in the presence of the woman he loves . . .

The waiter is in front of the man with the pizza.

"Having lunch, eh?"

The traveler raises his serene gaze.

"That I am."

He gestures with his abundantly hairy hand.

Anguish gathers in Signor Dido's heart.

"You can't do that here!"

"Why not? It's very good. I had it made specially."

He points to the pizza, three fingers thick and already a good half eaten.

"Want to join me?"

"This is the dining car! It's forbidden!"

"Pizza's forbidden? Nobody told me."

He casts an innocent glance around.

"It should be written there." He points to the glass of the window.

"Enough chatter! Pizzas are not eaten here!"

"But they're really good. In the best restaurants . . ."

"Even in the king's palace, but here—no! This is the dining car!"

The second waiter is approaching.

Anguish clutches at Signor Dido's throat.

"No? . . . Who says so?"

The second waiter has joined the first waiter.

"Get up!"

A conflict is about to break out between the two waiters who are defending the privileges of the dining car and the man with the pizza.

What is going on in the latter's mind?

Signor Dido can bear it no longer. He gets up in a cloud of mist. Flees unsteadily. Finds himself back in the solitary compartment.

To the right, the mountains of Calabria unroll one after another and roll back up again; the sea to the left extends motionlessly under the sun. But Signor Dido now sees both the mountains and the sea in an eclipsed light.

Minutes pass.

Among his Dostoevskian memories, the memory of a character who is gnawed by anguish because he has fled the dining car without paying his bill is lacking. And yet . . .

Signor Dido makes up his mind.

He goes lurching down the corridor and through the accordion passage between the cars.

The dining car is empty. Gone is the elderly and thin married

ALBERTO SAVINIO

couple. Gone is the woman *aux foies blancs*. Gone is the man with the pizza.

No trace of a fight.

Signor Dido advances down the aisle.

At the far end of the car, behind a partition, the personnel of the dining car are eating.

"I left because I wasn't feeling very well . . . I'd like to pay . . ."

Sitting at the table are the two waiters, the cook with a white chef's hat on his head, and a fourth companion: the traveler with the pizza.

In the middle of the table, an enormous pizza. Its top red with tomatoes, silvery with anchovies.

Christmas.

134

Charon's Train

The train begins to move.

A solution.

To this accustomed solution we give no weight, and yet the solution of the train leaving is the model for far more serious solutions.

While the train stands in the station, both those who are about to leave and those who will remain have a "problem" to resolve.

Great uneasiness for the ones and for the others.

Death is likewise a solution, also preceded by a "problem." A greater solution than a train leaving, but of the same sort. *Mourir c'est partir beaucoup.*[1]

What more do those standing behind the compartment window and those waiting on the platform have to say to each other? Nothing. There is now too great a difference between them. More conscious of their own situation, more respectful of modesty, they will even avoid looking at each other.

The train leaves: all at once the situation is clarified. What matter if those of us in the same compartment don't know each other? Something unites us that is more profound than kinship itself: we are all passengers on Charon's ferry.

It is thus with the eye of an associate that I look at the traveler sitting across from me.

Can I have sympathy for this man of wood? this man on hinges? Certainly not. But what matter? The bonds that unite us, though unnoticeable to ourselves, are even stronger than love.

Brother!

My traveling companion is wearing a new suit. The jacket is perfect. The crease of the trousers is irreproachable. The shoes are new. New is the overcoat, which, before sitting down, the man folded carefully and laid on the luggage rack like a dear corpse. New is the shirt and ironed to perfection. New is the tie and masterfully knotted. New are the pigskin gloves.

Too new.

All at once, the reason for this rigid care in dressing is revealed to me.

My traveling companion, who knows when, who knows how, has lost his compactness, just as Peter Schlemihl, in his time, lost his shadow.[2] He is a man of sand. If not for the hard sheath of his clothes, he would pour out all over the floor of the car.

Nervous quivers run through him. Undressed, he would spray in all directions.

He will sleep dressed, like a fish boiled in a poacher.

Or maybe he doesn't sleep.

He holds an open book in the candelabra of his hands: *Le crime de Sylvestre Bonnard.*[3]

The title of a yellow book.

We cross a river in a clatter of scrap iron. My traveling companion turns to look. I see him in profile. A deep scar is carved on his right temple.

I understand.

A passage from the *Menippus* comes back to my mind:[4]

"Having come to the marsh, we barely managed to pass over, as Charon's bark was already full. Some with broken legs, some with split skulls, some with other limbs pierced."

Le crime de Sylvestre Bonnard is not a yellow book, and yet it was as a yellow book that I read it, in one breath, between midnight and dawn, in that far-off 1912, the year I met Apollinaire.

How sad memories are!

Behind the station of Pompeii, an enormous and squalid building: asylum for the children of prisoners.

• • •

In the dining car, the two places in front of me are empty.

A tiny woman arrives with brief little steps, when we've already come to the "main course." Her skirt at knee level, her legs swathed in white woolen knee stockings. She looks like a chorus girl from the *Elisir d'amore.*[5] She bows to me before sitting down.

"Spaghetti? Never. Meat? No again . . . An *omelette*: nothing else. And a glass of seltzer water: quickly!"

She fishes about in the bottom of a sort of little strongbox that she carries with her. With a thief's hand she takes out I don't know what kind of pill. She thinks I haven't seen her and pops it into her mouth. After it she sends the seltzer water.

A young girl joins the chorus girl on the seat next to her. Coarse skin. Not a trace of makeup. Yet from this innocent surface oozes I don't know what nastiness.

The chorus girl has a Chinese mask for a face. And she gradually goes off into delirium. Rivulets of sweat run down the furrows of her wrinkles.

She says as if singing:

"Shut me away in a convent . . . To see no one anymore . . . To think nothing anymore . . ."

"Just like you!" replies the young girl. "Just like you who wanted to found a convent of nudists!"

And she laughs with a laugh that turns one to ice.

Behind my back, the other half of the car is filled with a team of footballers. They are northerners and are going to play in the south.

In this storm of voices, I don't manage to fish out any sense.

It is barely four hours since we left, and our train is already a train of phantoms.

• • •

I go back to the compartment.

We're passing through Lucania.

This young man sitting here by the door is a law student. He said so himself to the gentleman sitting across from him. He is heading for Messina and will have to travel until seven in the evening.

En voyage sans livres, à la guerre sans musique . . .[6]

The young law student has brought no books with him, not even newspapers. Only the train schedule. An enormous, complete schedule.

He slips his forefinger between the leaves every now and then and reads the page he opens to.

It is his Bible.

• • •

Calabria.

Names unknown to my itineraries: Sapri, Capo Bonifati, Cetraro, Fuscaldo . . .

The train passes through these villages, but remains a stranger to them.

To put it better: it violates them.

• • •

Twilight.

A house every now and then. And all of them as if wounded.

Smoke above the roofs. They're cooking supper.

The smoke doesn't come from a chimney pot: it's the whole roof that smokes.

So, in the twilights of Ithaca, the roof smoked above the house of Ulysses.

• • •

After crossing the Strait—a little celebration—the train stops in the station of Messina.

It is night. One by one I have lost my companions on Charon's train. The last to get off was the student whose Bible is the train schedule.

I'm alone in the compartment. Through the open window . . .

What station are we in? Winter, here in the south, is an unsuitable season.

Through the open window, a loud, long smacking of kisses reaches me. Relations are meeting relations on the platform.

The kiss of relations is quite different from the kiss of lovers. It is the symbol of a kiss more than anything. It is like the kiss a general gives to a soldier, after the medal for valor.

But not here in the south. Here even the kiss between parents and children, even the kiss between brother and brother, even the kiss between relation and relation is a full, substantial kiss.

A kiss, they think here, would lose its meaning if it were not the effective transmission of that *ànemos*, that breath, which has given its name to *anima*, the soul.

Charon's train starts on its way again, for me, its last passenger.

The Night Watchman

I ARRIVE AT NIGHT. I FIND G. V. WAITING for me at the station. The automobile snakes its way up a rocky road. On reaching the summit, we go through an archway and stop in a courtyard surrounded by high walls.

Beyond the front door, I find myself in a long and dimly lit corridor. Choir stalls are lined up along the walls. Is it a hotel I've come to, or a convent?

At the end of the corridor, more corridors: one to the left, the other to the right.

I nod towards the corridor to the left:

"This way?"

A certain apprehension has seeped into my question. I realize it from G. V.'s reassuring tone.

"No, the other."

We take the one to the right.

Who was that figure up there?

At the end of the corridor to the left, at the head of a grand staircase, I had glimpsed a figure dressed half in black and half in white, upright and perfectly immobile, left hand raised in an oratorical gesture, pallid face framed in extremely black hair and an equally black beard.

A man or a statue?

I don't dare ask G. V.

And again corridor after corridor.

At last G. V. opens a door.

"Your room."

The door, dark and massive, closes behind me.

A dense silence surrounds me, encloses me on all sides: the supreme privilege of luxury hotels.

So here I am in famous Taormina.

And if in the act of paying the bill any astonishment should make itself seen, it is with full rights that the accounting expert will be able to say to you: "Yes, but between our clients and the world we interpose an ineffable mattress."

And that figure up there, at the head of the grand staircase?

• • •

Between nine and midnight, nothing noteworthy. I put myself in order, went to dinner in the dining room, stopped to speak with "the others."

At midnight I was back in my room.

• • •

I peeked out the door several times: now a distant noise, now a shadow at the end of the corridor . . .

When I finally set out for the grand stairway, it was one o'clock.

• • •

I didn't worry about walking softly: the thick carpets deadened all sound.

The fault of carpets: you don't hear footsteps approaching.

We ran into each other at the turning of a corridor.

"Sorry!"

"Sorry!"

The brim of his hat covered his eyes. The collar of his overcoat half hid his face. And the hotel was overheated.

I noticed despite these "precautions" that he had a beard.

It cost me quite an effort not to turn around.

The voice hit me in the back:

"Are you a guest at the hotel?"

"Yes, I arrived this evening. Why?"

"Oh, nothing . . . I'm the night watchman."

He drew his right hand from the pocket of his overcoat and touched the brim of his hat.

"Good night."

The black beard, the resemblance . . .

"One word!"

The man turned around.

"Aren't you hot in that overcoat? It's very hot in here."

"I also have to go out to the garden, to take a turn around the hotel."

Again he made as if to leave.

"Good night."

Could I let him go away? Take my suspicions with him?

"Tell me . . . Are there many guests?"

"Let's see . . . Three English people . . .[1] You'll have seen them in the dining room."

Indeed. While I was eating, three people were sitting a short distance from me: a woman and two men.

"She, they say, is a poetess."

I had examined her for a long time from my table. Extremely old, despite the chemical and above all the psychic treatment with which she sought to fend off, as too banal, the accounting of time.

The effort this lady makes, I had thought, is a problem of style.

Extremely old and extremely tall, and monumentally pyramidal.

I had admired her even more when she got up from the table and, slowly, abstractly, went diagonally across the dining room.

At the top of that enormous bell which moved with no apparent mechanism, the pear-shaped head culminated in a yellowish little cone, under which two silvery discs rounded: the eyes presumably and the contour of their sockets.

There followed a man who, for his part, had white eyes and purple cheeks: an extremely tall gentleman, flaxen and ageless, his body bent forward by an obvious ankylopoietic spondyloarthritis.

"Yes," the night watchman confirmed. "Her brother and a poet himself."

Third came a man who was younger but of the same stature, a sort of summary of the first two, and perhaps for that reason devoid of any vital substance of his own.

"Their secretary," the night watchman completed. "They live in a castle near London. But it's cold there now and they've come to Taormina . . . Hear that?"

"What?"

"That music . . . It's an American economist. He was a minister under Roosevelt. Now he's here on his honeymoon."

I stood listening: in the end I made out a very distant sizzle of guitars and mandolins.

"He wants to have a little orchestra outside his room playing Neapolitan songs for him. Sometimes he keeps them all night . . . You understand, when you've got the money . . ."

"In that case, I'd pay them not to play . . . Is that all your guests?"

"There's also an old Danish gentleman, but I don't know who he might be . . . The season really begins later, in January, and goes till the end of April."

The night watchman's gaze withdrew into itself and sank into memories.

"The season . . . Who knows if the real season will ever come back again? . . . This is a sacred place. No one has the privilege of enjoying sacred places today . . . These three English people? Creatures outside time. Looking at them, you understand the present politics of England . . . This economist is also outside time, though he's not English but American. An old man, and he goes on a honeymoon . . . And this surrounding himself with Neapolitan songs . . . Posthumous revenge on Mussolini . . . And he probably doesn't notice it himself . . . The last season in this divine place, in the whole geography of divine places, was in the time of the Kaiser. Guglielmone came up here once:[2] he discovered Taormina. That dangerous madman made a discovery every once in a while: now the yellow peril, now Ruggero Leoncavallo, now Taormina . . . Guglielmone started the First World War, which, among so many dead, also brought death to the season of the divine places . . . No, I don't impute to that poor imbecile the direct responsibility for this death. I mention Guglielmone as one marks a date. Those who, by a not so rare privilege, truly succeeded in overcoming the obligation to work, came up here to live a white life, as the gods once lived on Olympus. Not any more. Now even those who succeed in overcoming the obligation to work remain equally immersed in movement, which seizes, overturns, overthrows, transforms, and do not live a limpid life, a white life, but a life choked with mud. Movement is tragedy. Happiness is to feel no movement anymore and to forget it . . . To forget life . . . Will the season ever come back again to these divine places? . . . Who knows . . . And even if it comes back, the divine places will no longer be here, will no longer be these . . . Tragedy accelerates man's industry. Gripped by tragedy, men will construct such mechanisms as can take them far from our

planet . . . The future divine places will perhaps be on the planet
Mars . . ."

A night watchman who reasons like a modern-day Spengler,
an appearance that reminds me more and more of . . .

"There's something I'm curious about: this evening, arriving
at the hotel, I glimpsed an upright, immobile figure at the head of
a grand staircase. Is it a man or a statue?"

The night watchman looked fixedly at me and began to smile.

"How could it be a man? . . . It's a statue. The statue of a saint,
a reminder that this is an ex-convent."

We said good night.

I stood behind the door to my room, keeping watch.

I went out again and down the corridors.

At the head of the grand staircase I found neither man nor
statue: no one at all.

No Brakes

It is noon and Signor Dido is still in bed. Twelve chimes have rung out from the clock on the writing desk. Twelve golden chimes. This clock, which is a windup clock, Signor Dido calls "the pendulum." Signor Dido's mother also called it "the pendulum": the grand baroness, who returned fifteen years ago, with her vulture's eyes and her eagle's hands, to the Unity of All. Ancient errors rooted in the history of families. Errors which, at bottom, contain a profound rightness, a profound truth. How extirpate them now? And why extirpate them? Twelve golden chimes. The Pendulum. The Grand Baroness is no more. Signor Dido himself is old. And the golden voice of the Pendulum is as pure and flawless as ever. It will still be ringing when Signor Dido . . .

Professor Elvio, Signor Dido's attendant physician and personal friend, is sitting kitty-corner to Signor Dido's bedside. Signora Dido is sitting on the edge of the bed, her back englobed around an ample radius.

The position of a wife.

In bed, man is in an inferior position. Signor Dido is now in an inferior position, not only because he is in bed, but also because Signora Dido is weighing down the covers, as if squeezing him in a sack.

Signor Dido is unhappy.

He is unhappy because he is in bed; he is unhappy because Signora Dido is weighing down the covers, as if squeezing him in a sack; he is unhappy because Professore Elvio, his attendant physician and personal friend, is scrutinizing him through lenses rimmed with steel the way an examiner scrutinizes an ill-prepared student.

Why, when noon has struck, is Signor Dido still in bed?

The day before, in the late afternoon, Signor Dido attended the opening of a painter friend of his. At nine, a cold supper was prepared in the home of some friends of the painter, who have a villa outside Rome. It was raining; Signor Dido did not know the way.

In Signor Dido's automobile, Signora Dido placed herself in the back seat: to Signor Dido's right sat a woman who knew the way and had offered to act as guide. Wrapped in gray fur, she was a source of fascination.

They had to get to the Via Portuense, pass in front of the Forlanini, take the road to Fiumicino, and turn right onto a road called dell'Affogalàsino.

The night was dark; Rome and its periphery were dimly lit.

Signor Dido was just driving onto the Ponte dell'Industria. He stepped on the brake pedal, but his foot stepped on the accelerator at the same time. The motor gave a great roar.

Signor Dido was surprised: surprised and worried.

However, he said with a facetious look: "I'm becoming acromegalic. I'm growing feet like Primo Carnera:[1] when I step on the brakes, I step on the accelerator at the same time." And Signor Dido went off into half-lyrical, half-humorous variations on the theme of acromegalism, because the source of fascination who was sitting beside him on the narrow seat, that opalescent profile, that warmth, that perfume, stimulated his fantasy.

Signor Dido passed in front of the lights of the Forlanini, reached by ever more squint-eyed streets the road to Fiumicino, turned right onto dell'Affogalàsino, passed through a gate, climbed up the steep and deserted road of a park.

The cold supper was faithful to the model of cold suppers. Signor Dido ate standing up, in the midst of other standing eaters, holding the plate under his chin like a barber's basin, taking care not to be bumped, swallowing whole slices of roast beef at the risk of choking himself, because that equilibrist's position did not allow him the use of a knife.

• • •

When the cold supper was over, sharp and syncopated sounds rose up and overwhelmed the disorderly shouting; some couples embraced and turned around themselves in a restricted space. Their eyes were open, but their faces were asleep.

At midnight Signor Dido made a move to go home.

This time the distribution of places in the automobile was as follows: Signor Dido at the wheel; to his right Signora P. M., a well-known writer; in the back seat Signora Dido and, to her left, the famous writer M. B.

His foot on the pedal, the gearshift in third, Signor Dido started down the road through the park. The automobile began to pick up speed.

Signor Dido searched for the brake pedal with his foot. The pedal was no longer there.

• • •

It is noon and Signor Dido is still in bed.

The evening before, he and his companions having escaped unhurt from this fearful adventure (an adventure caused, as became known later, by a stripped bolt that had left the brake pedal in the condition of a milk tooth about to fall out), Signor Dido and

Signora Dido had reached home by means of luck. Signor Dido's nervous tension held out as far as the house. On the threshold of the house, Signor Dido collapsed.

Now Signor Dido is in bed. He is in bed and unhappy. He is unhappy because he is in bed; he is unhappy because Signora Dido's back is pinning him down under the covers; he is unhappy because he *feels himself a prey.*

Professore Elvio, his attendant physician and personal friend, has questioned him at length about shock and the effects of shock. But they were not sincere questions: they were insidious questions. Each of Professore Elvio's questions was intended to unmask Signor Dido, to make Signor Dido say things that he was concealing. Is a sick man then someone to be distrusted? . . . Signor Dido's answers fell on barren ground. Nothing on Professore Elvio's face betrayed it.

Signora Dido's face is worried. But behind the varnish of worry, Signora Dido is pleased, and Signor Dido knows it. Professore Elvio's incredulity *plays into her hand.* Signor Dido says that he is well? That he is ready to get up? Nonsense! The whole day in bed. And maybe tomorrow as well. And the day after, not in bed, but in an armchair.

Signor Dido is their prey: the prey of Signora Dido, the prey of Professore Elvio.

A fine illness that, under the veil of affectionate solicitude, of medical treatment, gives a virtuous appearance to predators!

Why does Signor Dido find death repugnant? Dead, a man becomes the total and definitive prey of those who are left alive. And he lies there: mum.

"Air! Air!"

Signora Dido believes in the restorative virtues of air.

"The window? . . . Too cold. But the door at least."

Nice Mattaglioni, the maid of all work in the Dido household, profits from the open door.

Nice Mattaglioni, short on personal life, loves mixing into the life of others.

Two particular features characterize Nice Mattaglioni: a boundless admiration for her own father, a small rural landowner and extemporaneous poet; and the practice of equivalences, which consists in opposing to any fact of someone else's a fact of her own.

"Poor signore!" murmurs Nice Mattaglioni, peeking shyly from the doorway at Signor Dido stretched out in bed. "These cars! Nothing but trouble! . . . Even my father. One evening he was coming home on his motorcycle. All of a sudden, *poom!* a tire blew: papa went flying into the fields. My mama, poor thing, lit one match after another looking for the pieces."

Signora Dido asks:

"Your father was blown to pieces?"

"No, he was fine."

How deny that the sources of fantasy well up from the people?

"Basta!" cries Signor Dido. "I won't be a prey anymore! I'll be like that cursed car: no brakes!"

So saying, Signor Dido throws the covers into the air and leaps out of bed. Signora Dido had been sitting on the edge: she finds herself sitting on the floor.

"Are you crazy? Get back in bed at once!"

Professor Elvio says nothing and stares through his lenses at the empty bed.

In pajamas and with the gait of a marionette, Signor Dido goes off down the corridor.

Man, in each of his acts, is sacred.

So thinks Nice Mattaglioni.

She looks at Signor Dido, in whom she sees her own father again, and murmurs: "The signore! . . . What a hero!"

A Mental Journey

SIGNOR DIDO RESIDES IN ROME. A few days ago he made a short trip to Milan. He went by train. And alone. Differently than had been planned.

It had been planned that Signor Dido would go to Milan by automobile and in the company of Signora T. More exactly, Signor Dido would have traveled from Rome to Milan in the automobile of Signora T., who owns a powerful automobile and drives it herself, with the same authority and the same skill with which Armida drove the dragons yoked to her chariot.[1]

The parallel between Signora T. and Armida is not fortuitous. Both are witches. The magic practiced by Signora T. is less sulphurous than that practiced by Armida, but to make up for that, it is more subtle and of greater range.

All the same, it has no power over internal combustion engines. The night before the planned trip to Milan, the engine in Signora T.'s automobile broke down. Signora T. left for Milan by train. Signor Dido also left for Milan by train.

In the capital of the ex-duchy, Signor Dido and Signora T. met. They visited an important exhibition of paintings together. They dined now in restaurants of international fame, now in eating places of local character but equally conspicuous as to price.

So it went for three days. At the end of the third day, Signora T. said to Signor Dido:

"Tomorrow I go back to Rome."

Signor Dido hesitated for a moment, but then said in his turn:

"I, too, go back to Rome tomorrow."

"I'm taking the 12:45 express," said Signora T.

"I'm also taking the 12:45 express," Signor Dido said in his turn, and it seemed to him that the voice of Echo was in his mouth.

"It's a good idea to reserve a place in the Pullman," Signora T. suggested.

"Do you think so?" asked Signor Dido. "I always find a place on the train."

And Signor Dido, trusting in his good railway star, did not reserve a place.

• • •

The next day, at the stroke of noon, Signor Dido went up the majestic stairs of the Milan station. He was slightly agitated. In Signor Dido's organism, psychic agitations influence the digestive system.

The train was standing in the station.

It was not the train Signor Dido was expecting. He was expecting a streamlined electric express, high of windows and warlike of armor plating. He found instead a train of cars antiquated in form and divided into compartments.

And the Pullmans? Where were the Pullmans?

Signor Dido occupied the two window seats in a first-class compartment. On the seat facing in the direction of the trip and destined for Signora T., Signor Dido placed his own beret: that beret with which, except in seasons that allowed one to go around bareheaded, he usually protected his baldness.

Signor Dido climbed down to the platform. The effects of

psychic agitation on his digestive system were increasing.

Signora T. came through the gate to the tracks at 12:43. She was escorted by two Herculeses in striped capes, bent under suitcases. She stopped by a car watched over by a uniformed employee and handed him a piece of paper.

As Signora T. was setting about climbing into the car watched over by the uniformed employee, Signor Dido said softly to her:

"I've saved two places in first class."

"But this one is the Pullman," said Signora T., continuing to climb in. "They've reserved a place for me."

"Ah, really?"

Signor Dido went up to the uniformed employee.

"Kindly give me a place on the Pullman." And so saying, Signor Dido patted the bulge of his wallet on his right buttock.

"All taken," replied the uniformed employee.

Signor Dido relayed the words of the uniformed employee to Signora T. He added:

"Let's try to meet in the dining car."

"Travelers in the Pullman," replied Signora T., "are served in their own places."

Signor Dido climbed down quickly. He caught hold of the door of his car as the train was already moving.

He ate alone.

When he went back to his compartment, he found the place destined for Signora T. occupied by a priest. He was sleeping peacefully, his lips rounded in the form of a kiss.

Signor Dido huddled on the seat. Through the window, between one cloud and the next, he glimpsed the stern but friendly face of Fate.

A piercing draft came through the window. Signor Dido shrank back against the seat. He began to think.

He thought:

Man, as a male, is an incomplete creature. Man finds his complement in woman, and forms with her that complete creature which the Greeks once represented in Hermaphroditos, and today is designated by the word Androgyne.

In youth, man sets about the acquisition of his complement by cynegetic means; in old age he sets about it by less violent means, as a sick man obtains a sick-nurse.

One must prepare oneself for the most ticklish situation. Remain perfectly defenseless. One must entrust oneself to safe hands, to eyes in which that scorn does not appear which is in the hunter's look at his prey.

Only the most trustworthy hands can return us to the Great Mother from whom we have all come. *Hic natus hic situs est.*[2]

Signor Dido thought trustingly of the hands of Signora Dido.

The lights of Rome shone in the night.

The train stopped in the station.

Signor Dido was slow to get off.

He plunged into the sea of passengers, just as, when a child, in case of danger, he had gone to hide himself behind the divan in the living room.

The Disappearance of Signor Dido

Up bright and early!

It is seven-thirty.

The bus is parked in front of the hotel entrance.

The matutinal and punctual are already sitting in the bus. The rear door gapes open, waiting for the latecomers.

"And Massimo? And Paola?"

"Paola announced that she's tired and isn't coming. Here's Massimo now."

Massimo, ancient, tiny, with his trumpet-like nose, comes scurrying on little steps under his trailing overcoat. A dozen men and women, furred, cloaked, scarfed, pour out the door of the hotel and swarm towards him.

"Here's Massimo! Here's Massimo!"

The company fans out, moves with the movement of a farandole, draws Massimo in, bears him with their group right up to the bus.

They are all people of a certain age, some even quite old, but today they behave like little children. Who knows? The early rising, the excursion, that puerility which is so intimately connected with senility . . . They get into the bus a few at a time, pushing each other from below, pulling each other from above, laughing and vying with each other in high spirits.

157

Spirits . . .

"Are we all here? Nobody missing?"

"Nobody!"

The thud of the closing door, the rasp of the gearbox, and they're off! The entire jury of the poetry prize,[1] with a constellation of the committee members' wives, though the stars were in truth a little spent, escorted by journalists and photographers, excited and shouting, sets out for Mongibello.[2]

Italy, as we know, sends up a whole garden of prizes each season: prizes for poetry, prizes for painting, prizes for fiction.

The most celebrated names of national tourism, and the less celebrated as well, think to make themselves still more celebrated by offering conspicuous cash prizes to poets, painters, fiction writers, and bestowing the awards and laurels amidst the whirl of ostentatious evenings.

Even Signor Dido is occasionally called upon to serve on a prize committee, though his service is usually very discreet—so discreet as to become inoperative.

In the days prior to the awarding of the prize, the committee members' time is divided between the labors of the judging sessions and recreational excursions.

This trip to Mongibello is just such a recreational excursion.

The bus speeds for a stretch down the Messina–Catania road, turns right onto a road marked at the start by a sign saying ETNA, begins to snake its way up the mountain that stands like a beautiful pyramid of *marron glacé* whitened at the top by a bit of whipped cream, under which Enceladus sleeps a peaceful sleep, shaken now and then by frightening dreams.[3]

For Signor Dido, this excursion up Etna is more than anything else an on-the-spot investigation.

Signor Dido cannot say that he is not on good terms with his contemporaries, but he is on much better terms with some people of the past, and even of the remotest past.

One of them is Empedocles.[4]

Empedocles was a physicist and at the same time a poet. In other words, he did not separate the physical from the metaphysical. That is what makes Empedocles so pleasing to Signor Dido, because Signor Dido also thinks that there is no break between the physical and the metaphysical, and that the metaphysical is the direct and natural continuation of the physical.

Before this recreational excursion, Signor Dido had never been on Etna. He is quite pleased, therefore, to be approaching places that were the setting for one of the most important events in Empedocles' life—to wit, his death.

The bus, in which the shouting is beginning to die down and some heads are nodding, drives through Trecastagni, leaves behind the vineyards, the orange groves, the "gardens" bordered by prickly pears, and enters a black and motionless sea of old lava, less old lava, recent lava.

Of the death of Empedocles there are, as we know, several versions. Empedocles—Heraclides tell us—performed a sacrifice to which he invited several friends. After the banquet, the friends went to sleep under the trees: Empedocles remained alone at the banquet table, after which he disappeared.

Then there is the version of Hippobotus. "Empedocles, remaining alone, rose from the table and climbed up Etna. He threw himself into the crater in order to vanish from men's eyes and thus give greater credence to the rumors, already persistently going around, that he was a god. But the crater some time later spat up one of Empedocles' shoes, and returned it intact, because Empedocles wore bronze shoes."[5]

Mongibello, which could be contemplated from the hotel

terrace in all its breadth and height, disappeared from Signor Dido's sight now that he was on it. "Chateaubriand was right," thinks Signor Dido. "Mountains must be seen from a distance."

Now there is a lunar desert all around: the desert of a moon blackened by some ancient fire. Here and there a gigantic broom plant, a few pines closer to the effects of rust than of chlorophyll.

The first stop was at a shelter, the second at a hotel a little lower down, where the tables were set for a banquet.

The analogy struck Signor Dido.

A banquet then, a banquet now.

True, the sacrifice is missing. But is life itself not perhaps a sacrifice?

From in back came a quivering of strings, a banging of drums. Singers burst into the banquet room, the women in vests and skirts, the men with black bonnets hanging down their backs like socks.

The choruses of the singers were answered by the speeches of the tourists. A sort of Compar Alfio,[6] vibrating the sound with his tongue, his lips, his fingers, and his heart, performed a solo on the Jew's harp, which the tourists, at their tables, listened to gravely, their eyes shining and fixed on the void.

Neither the choruses, nor the speeches, nor even the Jew's harp succeeded in distracting Signor Dido from his Empedoclean meditations.

He thought:

"I, too, am now on Etna. I've seen what it's about. Interminable spaces, roads that never end. And we've done it by bus. How would it have been if we'd had to do it on foot? And after going all that way we've arrived here—here, barely fifteen hundred meters up. And they say that to reach the plateau, you have to climb another thirteen hundred meters. And to reach the top of the cone, where the crater opens, it's another four hundred and sixty meters. All right, there are lesser craters, but still . . . What sort of man was this Empedocles? And when he came up here he was no youngster: he was sixty years old, the same as me. What did he have for legs?"

Coffee was being served. The tourists signed the menu in turn, in memory of this magnificent Etnean day.

Though not usually very loquacious with his wife, Signor Dido communicated to Signora Dido his astonishment at the alpinistic abilities of Empedocles of Agrigentum.

He added: "And, after all, why couldn't I do the same thing Empedocles did?"

Signora Dido replied: "Have you looked in the mirror?"

• • •

"Fall in!" piped the boyish voice of Signor Pino, a photographer attached to tourism and the group's leader.

Committee members, wives of committee members, journalists, photographers climbed back into the bus. Less brash now, and their voices more restrained.

"Are we all here? Nobody missing?"

A pause.

"Professore Dido is missing . . . Where is Professore Dido?"

Signor Dido was not in the banquet room, nor in the intimate places of the hotel, nor in the pinewood below the hotel, crisscrossed by frightened parties of "processionaries."

Signora Dido, however reluctantly, made up her mind to speak.

"We were at the table. My husband said to me: 'Empedocles, after the banquet, got up from the table and went to throw himself into the crater of Etna.' He added: 'After all, why couldn't I do what Empedocles did?'"

161

There was a chorus of laughter.

"Always a great jester, that Dido," shouted Professore Ciurlo. "Your husband was joking, as usual. Get in, Signora, get in! You'll see, we'll find him on the way down."

But Signora Dido did not want to get into the bus.

"No, I'll stay. If need be, I'll take another bus. Anyway, there's a hotel up here. If I want, I can even spend the night."

The bus started down. Signora Dido, left alone, began to climb.

The road was black; black was the land all around. Even the air was beginning to turn black.

"Dido! . . . Didooo! . . ."

Night fell, and Signora Dido went on climbing.

"Didooo! . . ."

And she thought: "He's always like that. He says it and means it . . . I know him . . . And the others think he's joking . . .

"Didooo! . . ."

Notes

Signor Dido's Afternoon

1. *professore*: The honorific titles *professore* and *dottore* are commonly used in Italy as a show of respect (or ironic respect), even for people who are not professors, doctors, or university graduates. Both Savinio and Signor Dido comment on that habit in several of the stories that follow.

2. Tòmbolo: A town between Pisa and Livorno where American troops were stationed after the liberation of Italy in May 1945.

3. Alfieri-style: Count Vittorio Alfieri (1749–1803), poet and playwright, was the author of numerous tragedies, satires, comedies, and a book of memoirs. At the age of forty-eight, despite an aversion for grammar, he taught himself ancient Greek

A Visit from K . . .

1. *birotae . . . dixit*: Latin, meaning "A two-wheeler sped by burning liquid (the Pontiff has spoken)."

2. D'Annunzio: The poet Gabriele D'Annunzio (1863–1938) began as a symbolist and "decadent" but after the First World War became a political figure of strong nationalist tendencies, who had considerable influence on Italian fascism. He was in every way the opposite of Savinio, who often refers to him with playful sarcasm.

3. Vienna . . . The Sacher restaurant: The Prater ("the Meadow") is a large public park in Vienna; Franz Joseph I (1830–1916) was the Austrian emperor; the Sacher is the most famous restaurant in Vienna, located in the Hotel Sacher.

4. *d'antan*: French for "yesteryear," with the overtones of François Villon's refrain *Mais où sont les neiges d'antan*? ("But where are the snows of yesteryear?").

5. Vincenzo Gemito: Gemito (1852–1929) was a sculptor, painter, draftsman, and goldsmith, born in poverty in Naples and largely self-taught. Savinio considered him a major artist.

Muse

1. Fragson . . . the Alhambra: The Alhambra was the most famous music hall in Paris, showcasing in its long history virtually all the stars of popular music and jazz from both sides of the Atlantic. Contrary to Savinio's belief, it continued to exist until 1967. Harry Fragson (1869–1913—Savinio mistakenly says 1914), a British-born Parisian music-hall singer, was perhaps the most popular performer at the Alhambra before his untimely death; it was estimated that his funeral, which Savinio goes on to describe, was attended by some 50,000 people.

2. *Menin . . . ardori*: The first two phrases are the opening invocations of the Iliad ("Sing, Goddess, the anger . . .") and the Odyssey ("Sing in me, Muse, of that man . . ."); the third line is from the invocation to the muse at the start of *Jerusalem Delivered*, an epic poem by Torquato Tasso (1544–1595): "You breathe heavenly ardors into my breast."

3. Stendhal . . . *Pages d'Italie*: Stendhal was the pen name of the French novelist and essayist Marie-Henri Beyle (1783–1842), who wrote his "pages about Italy" in 1818. In an article from 1950, Savinio referred to Stendhal as *mio autore preferito*, "my favorite writer."

Family

1. *Heureusement . . . femmes*: "It is fortunate that, in so profoundly antifeminist a country, there are still a few of us who uphold the rights of women."

2. Alcestis . . . Samuel: This speech comes from Savinio's play *Alcesti di Samuele* ("The Alcestis of Samuel"), in which the story of Alcestis is transposed to the conditions of Nazi Germany and the role of Hercules is given to Franklin Delano Roosevelt. The play was produced in the 1949–1950 season at the Piccolo Teatro da Milano, directed by the young Giorgio Strehler.

A Head Goes Flying

1. Alcinean: From Alcinous of Drepane, who hospitably received Jason and Medea when they fled from Colchis.

2. *tailleurs*: French for "pants suits."

Orpheus the Dentist

1. *Agenzia Fix*: Savinio's radio opera, *Agenzia Fix*, was first broadcast by Radio Audizioni Italiane in 1950, directed by Carlo Maria Giulini.

2. Marius de Zayas . . . Apollinaire . . . *Tiresias*: The Mexican artist, writer, and gallery owner Marius de Zayas (1880–1961) moved to New York as a young man and collaborated with the photographer Alfred Stieglitz, owner of the gallery 291. Scouting for new work in Paris in 1914, de Zayas met the poet Guillaume Apollinaire (1880–1918) and the young Savinio. Apollinaire's two-act comedy, *The Breasts of Tiresias*, written in 1903, was first performed in 1917; Francis Poulenc's operatic version premiered in Paris in 1947.

3. Casimir Delavigne: In the wake of Napoleon's debacle, the French poet and playwright Casimir Delavigne (1793–1843) wrote patriotic political verses and plays which brought him considerable fame in his lifetime. His play *Louis XI* was written in 1832.

The Bearded Gentleman

1. Little Shrimp: Little Shrimp (Minuzzolo in Italian) is the eight-year-old hero of a book of the same title by Carlo Collodi (1826–1890), a precursor of the author's more famous *Adventures of Pinocchio*.

The Small Plate

1. *univira*: Latin for a "one-man woman," i.e., a woman married only once.

2. Phryne: The reference is to artistic portrayals of the trial of the Athenian courtesan Phryne. She was about to be condemned for a capital offense when her lawyer removed her robe as she stood

before the jurors. They were so struck by her beauty that, in fear of Aphrodite, they acquitted her.

A Strange Family

1. "Dottore": See note 1 to "Signor Dido's Afternoon."

2. Topo: A shortened form of Topolino ("Little Mouse"), nickname of the smallest model of Fiat.

The Feeling of Ravenna

1. Nastagio degli Onesti . . . dinner: Nastagio degli Onesti is the hero of a tale from the *Decameron*, by Giovanni Boccaccio (1313–1375), which includes a vision, witnessed by Nastagio's dinner guests, of a naked damsel being pursued through the forest of Chiassi by hounds and an angry horseman.

2. Honorius: Born in 384 ad, Honorius became emperor of Rome at the age of eleven, under the protection of the general Stilicho, and ruled until his death in 423. It was he who, in the face of repeated barbarian invasions, moved the imperial capital to Ravenna. In 410, Alaric, king of the Visigoths, sacked Rome.

Five Trees

1. Vera Cacciatore Signorelli: Vera Cacciatore, née Signorelli (1911–2004), was the curator of the Keats-Shelley House museum in Rome from 1933 to 1979. She was married to the poet Edoardo Cacciatore.

2. Oh, sie, Spassmacher!: "Oh, you joker!"

3. Los . . . her!: "Come on, boys! Bring Signor Dido's painting here!"

A Villa in Rapallo

1. *une seconde jeunesse*: "a second childhood."

2. *rentiers*: French term for people who live on private income, dividends, and so on.

3. Mister Liberty: In English in the original.

The Health Spa

1. Luca Signorelli . . . Orvieto: The frescoes of the Last Judgment in the cathedral of Orvieto are the most important works of the painter Luca Signorelli (1445–1523), a disciple of Piero della Francesca.

2. He will . . . form: Inferno VI: 98: *Ripigliera sua carne et sua figura.*

3. "Drop it": *Lassa perda* in the original, the Roman dialect form of the standard Italian *Lascia perdere.*

4. metaphysical painting: In their youth (1909–1920), Savinio was the main theorist and his brother, Giorgio de Chirico, the main practitioner of what they called *la pittura metafisica.* The short-lived movement also included Mario Sironi, Carlo Carrà, Giorgio Morandi, and others.

The Kiss

1. Roberto Bracco: Roberto Bracco (1861–1943), a Neapolitan journalist, was also a major dramatist, deeply influenced by the realism of Ibsen. Largely forgotten now, he was considered several times for the Nobel Prize. His outspoken opposition to fascism made it impossible for his work to be staged or published after 1929.

2. These organs . . . below: Laurence Binyon's translation of Paradiso 2: 121–123: *Questi organi del mondo così vanno, / Come tu vedi omai, di grado in grado, / Che di su prendono, e di sotto fanno.*

3. So . . . two does: Binyon's translation of Paradiso 4: 6: *Sì si starebbe un cane intra due dame.*

4. *chien . . . quilles*: "a dog in a game of skittles."

The Pizza

1. *Elle a les foies blancs*: "She is lily-livered."

Charon's Train

1. *Mourir . . . beaucoup*: In his *Rondel de l'adieu* ("Rondeau of Farewell"), the poet Edmond Haraucourt (1856–1941) wrote the

sentimental line *Partir, c'est mourir un peu* ("To leave is to die a little"), to which the humorist Alphonse Allais (1854–1905) appended the line Savinio quotes: "To die is to leave a lot."

2. Peter Schlemihl: "The Miraculous Story of Peter Schlemihl" (1814), by Adelbert von Chamisso (1781–1838), tells of how Peter Schlemihl sold his shadow to the devil in exchange for an inexhaustible sack of gold.

3. *Le Crime de Sylvestre Bonnard*: A novel by the French poet and novelist Anatole France (1844–1924).

4. *Menippus*: The passage that follows comes from the dialogue *Menippus*, by the satirist and itinerant teacher Lucian of Samosata (ca. 120–180 AD).

5. *Elisir d'amore*: An opera by Gaetano Donizetti (1797–1848), one of the leading composers of bel canto.

6. *En voyage . . . musique*: "Traveling without books, going to war without music . . ." (source not found).

The Night Watchman

1. Three English people: The description that follows is suggestive of the poets Edith and Osbert Sitwell and Osbert's lover David Horner, who stayed in Taormina in 1952.

2. Guglielmone: i.e., "Big William." The reference is to the title of a famous caricature of Kaiser Wilhelm II by the Italian socialist writer and artist Gabriele Galantara (1867–1937).

No Brakes

1. Primo Carnera: Primo Carnera (1906–1967) was a world heavyweight boxing champion famous for his massive size.

A Mental Journey

1. Armida: In Tasso's *Jerusalem Delivered* (see note 2 to "Muse"), Armida is a Saracen witch who tries to prevent the crusaders from taking Jerusalem; she plans to murder the brave Christian soldier Rinaldo but instead falls in love with him, unhappily as it turns out.

(In one of his variations on the names of Signor Dido's children, Savinio calls them Armida and Rinaldo. Elsewhere he calls them Agnese and Rodolfino. The real names of Savinio's own children are Angelica and Ruggero, after characters in another Italian epic, Ariosto's *Orlando Furioso*.)

2. *Hic . . . est*: Latin, meaning "Here you were born, here you lie."

The Disappearance of Signor Dido

1. the poetry prize: That is, the prestigious Etna-Taormina International Poetry Prize, awarded in the decades following the Second World War.

2. Mongibello: An alternative name for Mount Etna, an active volcano located near the east coast of Sicily, between Taormina and Catania.

3. Enceladus . . . dreams: Enceladus belonged to the race of giants produced by the earth goddess Gaia, fertilized by drops of blood from the castrated Uranus. In the fight between the giants and the Olympian gods, Enceladus was wounded by a huge missile hurled by Athena, which turned him into the island of Sicily. The volcano's fires are said to be his sighs and the tremors his rolling in pain from his wound.

4. Empedocles: The pre-Socratic philosopher Empedocles (ca. 490–430 BC) was a native of Agrigento, then a Greek settlement in Sicily. He is thought to have been the last Greek philosopher to write his works in verse.

5. Heraclides . . . Hippobotus: The philosopher Heraclides Ponticus (ca. 390–310 BC), who studied under Plato in Athens, wrote on a wide variety of subjects. Hippobotus (ca. 200 BC) was a historian of philosophy and philosophers; his works, including the account of Empedocles' death, are frequently quoted by Diogenes Laertius (third century AD) in his *Lives of the Eminent Philosophers*.

6. Compar Alfio: A rich merchant and betrayed husband, who sings a famous aria in the opera *Cavalleria Rusticana*, by Pietro Mascagni (1863–1945).